Shakespeare's Legal Acquirements

SALZWASSER
VERLAG

John Lord Campbell

Shakespeare's Legal Acquirements

Reprint of the original, first published in 1859.

1st Edition 2023 | ISBN: 978-3-37513-818-9

Verlag (Publisher): Salzwasser Verlag GmbH, Zeilweg 44, 60439 Frankfurt, Deutschland
Vertretungsberechtigt (Authorized to represent): E. Roepke, Zeilweg 44, 60439 Frankfurt, Deutschland
Druck (Print): Books on Demand GmbH, In de Tarpen 42, 22848 Norderstedt, Deutschland

SHAKESPEARE'S

LEGAL ACQUIREMENTS CONSIDERED.

SHAKESPEARE'S

LEGAL ACQUIREMENTS

CONSIDERED.

By JOHN LORD CAMPBELL, LL.D., F.R.S.E.

IN

A LETTER TO J. PAYNE COLLIER, Esq., F.S.A.

"Thou art *clerkly*, thou art *clerkly!*"
Merry Wives of Windsor.

LONDON:
JOHN MURRAY, ALBEMARLE STREET.
1859.

PREFACE.

WHEN my old and valued friend, Mr. Payne Collier, received the following Letter, which I wrote with a view to assist him in his Shakespearian lucubrations, he forthwith, in terms which I should like to copy if they were not so complimentary, strongly recommended me to print and publish it in my own name,—intimating that I might thus have "the glory of placing a *stone* on the lofty CAIRN of our immortal bard." If he had said a "*pebble*," the word would have been more appropriate. But the hope of making any addition, even if infinitesimally small, to this great national monument, is enough to induce me to follow my friend's advice, although I am aware that by the attempt I shall be exposed to some peril. In pointing out Shakespeare's frequent use of law-phrases, and the strict propriety with which he always applies them, the CHIEF JUSTICE may be likened to the COBBLER, who, when shown the masterpiece of a great painter, representing the Pope surrounded by an interesting historical group, could not be prevailed upon to notice any beauty in the painting, except the skilful structure of a slipper worn by his Holiness.

Nevertheless I may meet with kinder critics, and some may think it right to countenance any effort to bring about a "fusion of Law and Literature," which, like "Law and Equity," have too long been kept apart in England.

Stratheden House, Jan. 1, 1859.

CONTENTS.

SHAKESPEARE'S
LEGAL ACQUIREMENTS CONSIDERED.

To J. Payne Collier, Esq.,

Riverside, Maidenhead, Berks.

Hartrigge, Jedburgh, N. B.,
September 15*th*, 1858.

My dear Mr. Payne Collier,

Knowing that I take great delight in Shakespeare's plays, and that I have paid some attention to the common law of this realm, and recollecting that both in my 'Lives of the Chancellors,' and in my 'Lives of the Chief Justices,' I have glanced at the subject of Shakespeare's legal acquirements, you demand rather peremptorily my opinion upon the question keenly agitated of late years, whether Shakespeare was a clerk in an attorney's office at Stratford before he joined the players in London?

From your indefatigable researches and your critical acumen, which have thrown so much new light upon the career of our unrivalled dramatist, I say, with entire sincerity, that there is no one so well qualified as yourself to speak authoritatively in this controversy, and I observe that in both the editions of your 'Life of Shakespeare' you are strongly inclined to the belief that the author of 'Hamlet' was employed some years in engrossing deeds, serving writs, and making out bills of costs.

However, as you seem to consider it still an open question, and as I have a little leisure during this long vacation, I cannot refuse to communicate to you my sentiments upon the subject, and I shall be happy if, from my professional knowledge and experience, I can afford you any information or throw out any hints which may be useful to you hereafter. I myself, at any rate, must derive some benefit from the task, as it will for a while drive from my mind the recollection of the wranglings of Westminster Hall. In literary pursuits should I have wished ever to be engaged,—

> "Me si fata meis paterentur ducere vitam
> Auspiciis, et sponte meâ componere curas."

Having read nearly all that has been written on Shakespeare's *ante-Londinensian* life, and carefully examined his writings with a view to obtain internal evidence as to his education and breeding, I am obliged to say that to the question you propound no positive answer can very safely be given.

Were an issue tried before me as Chief Justice at the Warwick assizes, "whether William Shakespeare, late of Stratford-upon-Avon, gentleman, ever was clerk in an attorney's office in Stratford-upon-Avon aforesaid," I should hold that there is evidence to go to the jury in support of the affirmative, but I should add that the evidence is very far from being conclusive, and I should tell the twelve gentlemen in the box that it is a case entirely for their decision,—without venturing even to hint to them, for their guidance, any opinion of my own. Should they unanimously agree in a verdict either in the affirmative or negative, I do not think that the court, sitting *in banco*, could properly set it aside and grant a new trial. But the probability is (particularly if the trial were by a special jury of Fellows of the Society of Antiquaries) that, after they had been some hours in deliberation, I should receive a message from them—"*there is no chance of our agreeing, and therefore we wish to be discharged;*" that having sent for them into court, and read them a lecture on the duty imposed upon them by law of being unanimous, I should be obliged to order them to be locked up for the night; that having sat up all night without eating or drinking, and "without fire, candle-light excepted," * they would come into court

* These are the words of the oath administered to the bailiff into whose custody the jurymen are delivered. I had lately to deter-

next morning pale and ghastly, still saying "*we cannot agree,*" and that, according to the rigour of the law, I ought to order them to be again locked up as before till the close of the assizes, and then sentence them to be put into a cart, to accompany me in my progress towards the next assize town, and to be shot into a ditch on the confines of the county of Warwick.

Yet in the hope of giving the gentlemen of the jury a chance of escaping these horrors, to which, according to the existing state of the law, they would be exposed, and desiring, without departing from my impartiality, to assist them in coming to a just conclusion, I should not hesitate to state, with some earnestness, that there has been a great deal of misrepresentation and delusion as to Shakespeare's opportunities when a youth of acquiring knowledge, and as to the knowledge he had acquired. From a love of the incredible, and a wish to make what he afterwards accomplished actually miraculous, a band of critics have conspired to lower the condition of his father, and to represent the son, when approaching man's estate, as still almost wholly illiterate. We have been

---

mine whether gas-lamps could be considered "candle-light." *In favorem vitæ*, I ventured to rule in the affirmative; and, the night being very cold, to order that the lamps should be liberally supplied with gas, so that, directly administering *light* according to law, they might, contrary to law, incidentally administer *heat*.

told that his father was a butcher in a small provincial town; that "pleasant Willy" was bred to his father's business; that the only early indication of genius which he betrayed was his habit, while killing a calf, eloquently to harangue the bystanders; that he continued in this occupation till he was obliged to fly the country for theft; that arriving in London a destitute stranger, he at first supported himself by receiving pence for holding gentlemen's horses at the theatre; that he then contrived to scrape an acquaintance with some of the actors, and being first employed as prompter, although he had hardly learned to read, he was allowed to play some very inferior parts himself;—and that without any further training he produced 'Richard III.,' 'Othello,' 'Macbeth,' and 'King Lear.' But, whether Shakespeare ever had any juridical education or not, I think it is established beyond all doubt that his father was of a respectable family, had some real property by descent, married a coheiress of an ancient house, received a grant of armorial bearings from the Heralds with a recognition of his lineage, was for many years an Alderman of Stratford, and, after being intrusted by the Corporation to manage their finances as Chamberlain, served the office of Chief Magistrate of the town. There are entries in the Corporation books supposed to indicate that at one period of his life he was involved in pecuniary difficulties; but this did not detract from his gentility, as is proved by the subsequent confirmation of his armorial bearings, with a slight alteration in his quarterings,—and he seems still to have lived respectably in Stratford or the neighbourhood.* That he was, as has been recently asserted, a glover, or that he ever sold wool or butcher's meat, is not proved by anything like satisfactory evidence;—and, at any rate, according to the usages of society in those times, occasional dealings whereby the owner of land disposed of part of the produce of it by retail were reckoned quite consistent with the position of a squire. At this day, and in our own country, gentlemen not unfrequently sell their own hay, corn, and cattle, and on the Continent the high nobility are well

* I am aware of your suggestion in your 'Life of Shakespeare,' that the first grant of arms to the father was at a subsequent time, when the son, although he had acquired both popularity and property, was, on account of his profession (then supposed to be unfit for a gentleman), not qualified to bear arms. But the "Confirmation" in 1596 recites that a patent had been before granted by Clarencieux Cooke to John Shakespeare, when chief magistrate of Stratford, and, as a ground for the Confirmation, that this original patent had been sent to the Heralds' Office when Sir William Dethick was Garter King-at-Arms. Against this positive evidence we lawyers should consider the negative evidence, that, upon search, an entry of the first grant is not found, to be of no avail: and there could be no object in forging the first grant, as an original grant in 1596 would have been equally beneficial both to father and son.

pleased to sell by the bottle the produce of their vineyards.

It is said that the worthy Alderman could not write his own name. But the fac simile of the document formerly relied upon to establish this [an order, dated 29th Sept., 7 Eliz., for John Wheeler to take upon himself the office of Bailiff, signed by nineteen aldermen and burgesses] appears to me to prove the contrary, for the name of Iohn Shackspér is subscribed in a strong, clear hand, and the *mark*, supposed to be his, evidently belongs to the name of Thomas Dyxun in the line below.* You tell us, in your latest edition, of the production of two new documents before the Shakespeare Society, dated respectively 3rd and 9th Dec., 11 Eliz., which, it is said, if John Shakespeare could have written, would have been signed by him,—whereas they only bear his mark. But in my own experience I have known many instances of documents bearing a mark as the signature of persons who could write well, and this was probably much more common in illiterate ages, when documents were generally authenticated by a seal. Even if it were demonstrated that John Shakespeare had not been "so well brought up that

* See that most elaborate and entertaining book, Knight's 'Life of Shakspere,' 1st ed., p. 16.

he could write his name," and that "he had a mark to himself like an honest, plain-dealing man,"—considering that he was born not very long after the wars of the Roses, this deficiency would not weigh much in disproving his wealth or his gentility. Even supposing him to have been a genuine marksman, he was only on a par in this respect with many persons of higher rank, and with several of the most influential of his fellow townsmen. Of the nineteen Aldermen and burgesses who signed the order referred to, only seven subscribe their names with a pen, and the High Bailiff and Senior Alderman are among the marksmen.

Whatever may have been the clownish condition of John Shakespeare, that the "Divine Williams" (as the French call our great dramatist) received an excellent school education can hardly admit of question or doubt. We certainly know that he wrote a beautiful and business-like hand, which he probably acquired early. There was a free grammar school at Stratford, founded in the reign of Edward IV., and reformed by a charter of Edward VI. This school was supplied by a succession of competent masters to teach Greek and Latin; and here the sons of all the members of the corporation were entitled to gratuitous instruction, and mixed with the sons of the neighbouring gentry. At such grammar schools, generally speaking, only a smattering of Greek was to be acquired, but the boys were thoroughly grounded in Latin grammar, and were rendered familiar with the most popular Roman classics. Shakespeare must have been at this school at least five years. His father's supposed pecuniary difficulties, which are said to have interrupted his education, did not occur till William had reached the age of 14 or 15, when, according to the plan of education which was then followed, the sons of tradesmen were put out as apprentices or clerks, and the sons of the more wealthy went to the university. None of his school compositions are preserved, and we have no authentic account of his progress; but we know that at these schools boys of industry and genius have become well versed in classical learning. Samuel Johnson said that he acquired little at Oxford beyond what he had brought away with him from Lichfield Grammar School, where he had been taught, like Shakespeare, as the son of a burgess; and many from such schools, without further regular tuition, have distinguished themselves in literature.

It is said that "the boy is the father of the man;" and knowing the man, we may form a notion of the tastes and habits of the boy. Grown to be a man, Shakespeare certainly was most industrious, and showed an insatiable thirst for knowledge. We may therefore fairly infer, that from early infancy he instinctively availed himself of every opportunity of mental culture,—

> "What time, where lucid Avon stray'd,
> To him the mighty mother did unveil
> Her awful face :—the dauntless child
> Stretched forth his little arms, and smiled."

The grand difficulty is to discover, or to conjecture with reasonable probability, how Shakespeare was employed from about 1579, when he most likely left school, till about 1586, when he is supposed to have gone to London. That during this interval he was merely an *operative*, earning his bread by manual labour, in stitching gloves, sorting wool, or killing calves, no sensible man can possibly imagine. At twenty-three years of age, although he had not become regularly learned as if he had taken the degree of M.A. at Oxford or Cambridge, after disputing in the schools *de omni scibili et quolibet ente*,—there can be no doubt that, like our Scottish BURNS, his mind must have been richly cultivated, and that he had laid up a vast stock of valuable knowledge and of poetical imagery, gained from books, from social intercourse, and from the survey of nature. Whoever believes that when Shakespeare was first admitted to play a part in the Blackfriars Theatre his mind was as unfurnished as that of the stolid 'Clown' in the 'Winter's Tale,' who called forth a wish from his own father that "there were no age between ten and three and twenty," will readily give credit to all the most extravagant and appalling marvels of mesmerism, clairvoyance, table-turning, and spirit-rapping.

Of Shakespeare's actual occupations during these important years, when his character was formed, there is not a *scintilla* of contemporary proof; and the vague traditionary evidence which has been resorted to was picked up many years after his death, when the object was to startle the world with things strange and supernatural respecting him.—That his time was engrossed during this interval by labouring as a mechanic, is a supposition which I at once dismiss as absurd.

Aubrey asserts that from leaving school till he left Warwickshire Shakespeare was a schoolmaster. If this could be believed, it would sufficiently accord with the phenomena of Shakespeare's subsequent career, except the familiar, profound, and accurate knowledge he displayed of juridical principles and practice. Being a schoolmaster in the country for some years (as Samuel Johnson certainly was), his mental cultivation would have steadily advanced, and so he might have been prepared for the arena in which he was to appear on his arrival in the metropolis.

Unfortunately, however, the pedagogical theory is not only quite unsupported by evidence, but it is not consistent with established facts. From the registration of the baptism of Shakespeare's children, and other well authenticated circumstances, we know that he continued to dwell in Stratford, or the immediate neighbourhood, till he became a citizen of London: there was no other school in Stratford except the endowed grammar school, where he had been a pupil; of this he certainly never was master, for the unbroken succession of masters from the reign of Edward VI. till the reign of James I. is on record; none of the mob who stand out for Shakespeare being quite illiterate will allow that he was qualified to be usher; and there is no trace of there having been any usher employed in this school.

It may likewise be observed that if Shakespeare really had been a schoolmaster, he probably would have had some regard for the "order" to which he belonged. In all his dramas we have three schoolmasters only, and he makes them all exceedingly ridiculous. First we have Holofernes in 'Love's Labour 's Lost,' who is brought on the stage to be laughed at for his pedantry and his bad verses; then comes the Welshman, Sir Hugh Evans, in the 'Merry Wives of Windsor,' who, although in holy orders, has not yet learned to speak the English language; and last of all, Pinch, in the 'Comedy of Errors,' who unites the bad qualities of a pedagogue and a conjuror.

By the process of exhaustion, I now arrive at the only other occupation in which it is well possible to imagine that Shakespeare could be engaged during the period we are considering—that of an attorney's clerk—first suggested by Chalmers, and since countenanced by Malone, yourself, and others, whose opinions are entitled to high respect, but impugned by nearly an equal number of biographers and critics of almost equal authority, —without any one, on either side, having as yet discussed the question very elaborately.

It must be admitted that there is no established fact with which this supposition is not consistent. At Stratford there was, by royal charter, a court of record, with jurisdiction over all personal actions to the amount of 30*l.*, equal, at the latter end of the reign of Elizabeth, to more than 100*l.* in the reign of Victoria. This court, the records of which are extant, was regulated by the course of practice and pleading which prevailed in the superior courts of law at Westminster, and employed the same barbarous dialect, composed of Latin, English, and Norman-French. It sat every fortnight, and there were belonging to it, besides the Town-clerk, six attorneys, some of whom must have practised in the Queen's Bench and in Chancery, and have had extensive business in conveyancing. An attorney, steward of the Earl of Warwick, lord of the manor of Stratford, twice a year held a court-leet and view of frankpledge there, to which a jury was summoned, and at which constables were appointed and various presentments were made.

If Shakespeare had been a clerk to one of these

attorneys, all that followed while he remained at Stratford, and the knowledge and acquirements which he displayed when he came to London, would not only have been within the bounds of possibility, but would seem almost effect from cause—in a natural and probable sequence.

From the moderate pay allowed him by his master he would have been able decently to maintain his wife and children; vacant hours would have been left to him for the indulgence of his literary propensity; and this temporary attention to law might have quickened his fancy,—although a systematic, life-long devotion to it, I fear, may have a very different tendency. Burke eloquently descants upon the improvement of the mental faculties by juridical studies; and Warburton, Chatterton, Pitt the younger, Canning, Disraeli, and Lord Macaulay are a few out of many instances which might be cited of men of brilliant intellectual career who had early become familiar with the elements of jurisprudence.

Here would be the solution of Shakespeare's *legalism* which has so perplexed his biographers and commentators, and which Aubrey's tradition leaves wholly unexplained. We should only have to recollect the maxim that "the vessel long retains the flavour with which it has been once imbued." Great as is the knowledge of law which Shakespeare's writings display, and familiar as he appears to have been with all its forms and proceedings, the whole of this would easily be accounted for if for some years he had occupied a desk in the office of a country attorney in good business,—attending sessions and assizes,—keeping leets and law days,—and perhaps being sent up to the metropolis in term time to conduct suits before the Lord Chancellor or the superior courts of common law at Westminster, according to the ancient practice of country attorneys, who would not employ a London agent to divide their fees.*

---

* If Shakespeare really was articled to a Stratford attorney, in all probability during the five years of his clerkship he visited London several times on his master's business, and he may then have been introduced to the green room at Blackfriars by one of his countrymen connected with that theatre.

Even so late as Queen Anne's reign there seems to have been a prodigious influx of all ranks from the provinces into the metropolis in term time. During the preceding century Parliament sometimes did not meet at all for a considerable number of years; and being summoned rarely and capriciously, the "London season" seems to have been regulated, not by the session of Parliament, but by the law terms,—

"—— and prints before Term ends."—*Pope.*

While term lasted, Westminster Hall was crowded all the morning, not only by lawyers, but by idlers and politicians in quest of news. Term having ended, there seems to have been a general dispersion. Even the Judges spent their vacations in the country, having when in town resided in their chambers in the Temple or Inns of Court. The Chiefs were obliged to remain in town a day or two after term

On the supposition of Shakespeare having been an attorney's clerk at Stratford we may likewise see how, when very young, he contracted his taste for theatricals, even if he had never left that locality till the unlucky affair of Sir Thomas Lucy's deer. It appears from the records of the Corporation of Stratford, that nearly every year the town was visited by strolling companies of players, calling themselves "the Earl of Derby's servants," "the Earl of Leicester's servants," and "Her Majesty's servants." These companies are most graphically represented to us by the strolling

---

for Nisi Prius sittings; but the Puisnes were entirely liberated when proclamation was made at the rising of the court on the last day of term, in the form still preserved, that "all manner of persons may take their ease, and give their attendance here again on the first day of the ensuing term." An old lady very lately deceased, a daughter of Mr. Justice Blackstone, who was a puisne judge of the Common Pleas and lived near Abingdon, used to relate that the day after term ended, the family coach, with four black long-tailed horses, used regularly to come at an early hour to Serjeants' Inn to conduct them to their country house; and there the Judge and his family remained till they travelled to London in the same style on the essoin-day of the following term. When a student of law, I had the honour of being presented to the oldest of the judges, Mr. Justice Grose, famous for his beautiful seat in the Isle of Wight, where he leisurely spent a considerable part of the year, *more majorum*. To his question to me, "Where do you live?" I answered, "I have chambers in Lincoln's Inn, my Lord." "Ah!" replied he, "but I mean—*when term is over*."

players in 'Hamlet' and in the 'Taming of the Shrew.' The custom at Stratford was for the players on their arrival to wait upon the Bailiff and Aldermen to obtain a licence to perform in the town. The Guildhall was generally allotted to them, and was fitted up as a theatre according to the simple and rude notions of the age. We may easily conceive that Will Shakespeare, son of the chief magistrate who granted the licence, now a bustling attorney's clerk, would actually assist in these proceedings when his master's office was closed for the day; and that he might thus readily become intimate with the manager and the performers, some of whom were said to be his fellow townsmen. He might well have officiated as prompter, the duty said to have been first assigned to him in the theatre at the Black-friars. The travelling associations of actors at that period consisted generally of not more than from five to ten members; and when a play to be performed in the Guildhall at Stratford contained more characters than individuals in the list of strollers, it would be no great stretch of imagination to suppose that, instead of mutilating the piece by suppression, or awkwardly assigning two parts to one performer, "pleasant Willy's" assistance was called in; and our great dramatist may thus have commenced his career as an actor in his native town.

To prove that he had been bred in an attorney's

office, there is one piece of direct evidence. This is an alleged libel upon him by a contemporary—published to the world in his lifetime—which, if it do actually refer to him, must be considered as the foundation of a very strong inference of the fact.

Leaving Stratford and joining the players in London in 1586 or 1587, there can be no doubt that his success was very rapid; for, as early as 1589, he had actually got a share in the Blackfriars Theatre, and he was a partner in managing it with his townsman Thomas Green and his countryman Richard Burbadge. I do not imagine that when he went up to London he carried a tragedy in his pocket to be offered for the stage as Samuel Johnson did 'IRENE.' The more probable conjecture is, that he began as an actor on the London boards, and being employed, from the cleverness he displayed, to correct, alter, and improve dramas written by others, he went on to produce dramas of his own, which were applauded more loudly than any that had before appeared upon the English stage.

> "Envy does merit as its shade pursue;"

and rivals whom he surpassed not only envied Shakespeare, but grossly libelled him. Of this we have an example in 'An Epistle to the Gentlemen Students of the Two Universities, by Thomas Nash,' prefixed to the first edition of Robert Greene's 'MENAPHON' (which was subsequently called '*Greene's* ARCADIA'), —according to the title-page, published in 1589. The alleged libel on Shakespeare is in the words following, viz.:—

"I will turn back to my first text of studies of delight, and talk a little in friendship with a few of our trivial translators. It is a common practice now-a-days, amongst a sort of shifting companions that run through every art and thrive by none, to leave the trade of *Noverint*, whereto they were born, and busy themselves with the endeavours of art, that could scarcely Latinize their neck-verse if they should have need; yet English Seneca, read by candle-light, yields many good sentences, as *blood is a beggar*, and so forth; and if you intreat him fair, in a frosty morning, he will afford you whole *Hamlets*; I should say handfuls of tragical speeches. But O grief! *Tempus edax rerum*—what is that will last always? The sea exhaled by drops will in continuance be dry; and Seneca, let blood, line by line, and page by page, at length must needs die to our stage."

Now, if the *innuendo* which would have been introduced into the declaration in an action, "*Shakespeare* v. *Nash*," for this libel (—"thereby then and there meaning the said William Shakespeare"—) be made out, there can be no doubt as to the remaining *innuendo* "thereby then and there meaning that the said William Shakespeare had been an attorney's clerk, or bred an attorney."

In Elizabeth's reign deeds were in the Latin tongue;

and all deeds poll, and many other law papers, began with the words "NOVERINT universi per presentes"—"Be it known to all men by these presents that, &c." The very bond which was given in 1582, prior to the grant of a licence for Shakespeare's marriage with Ann Hathaway, and which Shakespeare most probably himself drew, commences "NOVERINT *universi per presentes.*" The business of an attorney seems to have been then known as "the trade of NOVERINT." Ergo, "these shifting companions" are charged with having abandoned the legal profession, to which they were bred; and, although most imperfectly educated, with trying to manufacture tragical speeches from an English translation of Seneca.

For completing Nash's testimony (*valeat quantum*) to the fact that Shakespeare had been bred to the law, nothing remains but to consider whether Shakespeare is here aimed at? Now, independently of the expressions "whole Hamlets" and "handfuls of tragical speeches," which, had Shakespeare's 'HAMLET' certainly been written and acted before the publication of Nash's letter, could leave no doubt as to the author's intention, there is strong reason to believe that the intended victim was the young man from Warwickshire, who had suddenly made such a sensation and such a revolution in the theatrical world. Nash and Robert Greene, the author of 'Menaphon' or 'Arcadia,' the work to which Nash's Epistle was appended, were very intimate. In this very epistle Nash calls Greene "sweet friend." It is well known that this Robert Greene (who, it must always be remembered, was a totally different person from Thomas Green, the actor and part proprietor of the Blackfriars Theatre) was one of the chief sufferers from Shakespeare being engaged by the Lord Chamberlain's players to alter stock pieces for the Blackfriars Theatre, to touch up and improve new pieces proposed to the managers, and to supply original pieces of his own. Robert Greene had been himself employed in this department, and he felt that his occupation was gone. Therefore, by publishing Nash's Epistle in 1589, when Shakespeare, and no one else, had, by the display of superior genius, been the ruin of Greene, the two must have combined to denounce Shakespeare as having abandoned "the trade of Noverint" in order to "busy himself with the endeavours of art," and to furnish tragical speeches from the translation of Seneca.

In 1592 Greene followed up the attack of 1589 in a tract called 'The Groatsworth of Wit.' Here he does not renew the taunt of abandoning "the trade of NOVERINT," which with Nash he had before made, but he pointedly upbraids Shakespeare by the nickname of *Shake-scene*, as "an upstart crow beautified with our feathers," having just before spoken of himself as "the man to whom actors had been previously beholding."

He goes on farther to allude to Shakespeare as one who "supposes he is as well able to bombast out a blank verse as the best of his predecessors," as "an absolute Johannes Factotum," and "in his own conceit the only SHAKE-SCENE in a country." In 1592 Robert Greene frankly complains that *Shake-scene* had undeservedly met with such success as to be able to drive him (Greene) and others similarly circumstanced from an employment by which they had mainly subsisted.* This evidence, therefore, seems amply sufficient to prove that there was a conspiracy between the two libellers, Nash and Robert Greene, and that Shakespeare was the object of it.

But I do not hesitate to believe that Nash, in 1589, directly alludes to 'HAMLET' as a play of Shakespeare, and wishes to turn it into ridicule. I am aware that an attempt has been made to show that there had been an edition of 'Menaphon' before 1589; but no copy of any prior edition of it, with Nash's Epistle appended to it, has been produced. I am also aware that 'Hamlet,' in the perfect state in which we now behold it, was not finished till several years after; but I make no doubt

* You no doubt recollect that Robert Greene actually died of starvation before his 'Groatsworth of Wit,' in which he so bitterly assailed *Shakespeare* as "Shake-scene," was published.

that before the publication of Nash's Epistle Shakespeare's first sketch of his play of 'Hamlet,' taken probably from some older play with the same title, had been produced upon the Blackfriars stage and received with applause which generated envy.

From the saying of the players, recorded by BEN JONSON, that Shakespeare never blotted a line, an erroneous notion has prevailed that he carelessly sketched off his dramas, and never retouched them or cared about them after. So far from this (contrary to modern practice), he often materially altered, enlarged, and improved them subsequently to their having been brought out upon the stage and having had a successful run. There is clear proof that he wrote and rewrote 'Hamlet,' 'Romeo and Juliet,' 'The Merry Wives of Windsor,' and several other of his dramas, with unwearied pains, making them at last sometimes nearly twice as long as they were when originally represented.

With respect to these dates it is remarkable that an English translation of Seneca, from which Shakespeare was supposed to have plagiarised so freely, had been published several years before Nash's Epistle;—and in the scene with the players on their arrival at Elsinore (if this scene appeared in the first sketch of the tragedy, as it probably did, from being so essential to the plot), Shakespeare's acquaintance with this author was proclaimed by the panegyric of Polonius upon the new company, for whom "SENECA could not be too heavy nor Plautus too light."

Therefore, my dear Mr. Payne Collier, in support of your opinion that Shakespeare had been bred to the profession of the law in an attorney's office, I think you will be justified in saying that the fact was asserted publicly in Shakespeare's lifetime by two contemporaries of Shakespeare, who were engaged in the same pursuits with himself, who must have known him well, and who were probably acquainted with the whole of his career.

I must likewise admit that this assertion is strongly corroborated by internal evidence to be found in Shakespeare's writings. I have once more perused the whole of his dramas, that I might more satisfactorily answer your question, and render you some assistance in finally coming to a right conclusion.

In 'The Two Gentlemen of Verona,' 'Twelfth Night,' 'Julius Cæsar,' 'Cymbeline,' 'Timon of Athens,' 'The Tempest,' 'King Richard II.,' 'King Henry V.,' 'King Henry VI. Part I.,' 'King Henry VI. Part III.,' 'King Richard III.,' 'King Henry VIII.,' 'Pericles of Tyre,' and 'Titus Andronicus'—fourteen of the thirty-seven dramas generally attributed to Shakespeare—I find nothing that fairly bears upon this controversy. Of course I had only to look for expressions and allusions that must be supposed to come from one who has been a professional lawyer. Amidst the seducing beauties of sentiment and language through which I had to pick my way, I may have overlooked various specimens of the article of which I was in quest, which would have been accidentally valuable, although intrinsically worthless.

However, from each of the remaining twenty-three dramas I have made extracts which I think are well worth your attention. These extracts I will now lay before you, with a few explanatory remarks,—which perhaps you will think demonstrably prove that your correspondent is a *lawyer*, AND NOTHING BUT A LAWYER.

I thought of grouping the extracts as they may be supposed to apply to particular heads of law or particular legal phrases, but I found this impracticable; and I am driven to examine *seriatim* the dramas from which the extracts are made. I take them in the order in which they are arranged, as "Comedies," "Histories," and "Tragedies," in the folio of 1623, the earliest authority for the whole collection.

The Merry Wives of Windsor.

In Act II. Sc. 2, where Ford, under the name of Master Brook, tries to induce Falstaff to assist him in his intrigue with Mrs. Ford, and states that from all the trouble and money he had bestowed upon her he had had no beneficial return, we have the following question and answer :—

> *Fal.* Of what quality was your love, then?
> *Ford.* Like a fair house built upon another man's ground ; so that *I have lost my edifice by mistaking the place where I erected it.*

Now this shows in Shakespeare a knowledge of the law of real property, not generally possessed. The unlearned would suppose that if, by mistake, a man builds a fine house on the land of another, when he discovers his error he will be permitted to remove all the materials of the structure, and particularly the marble pillars and carved chimney-pieces with which he has adorned it; but Shakespeare knew better. He was aware that, being fixed to the freehold, the absolute property in them belonged to the owner of the soil, and he recollected the maxim, *Cujus est solum, ejus est usque ad cœlum.*

Afterwards, in writing the second scene of Act IV., Shakespeare's head was so full of the recondite terms of the law, that he makes a lady thus pour them out, in a confidential *tête-à-tête* conversation with another lady, while discoursing of the revenge they two should take upon an old gentleman for having made an unsuccessful attempt upon their virtue :—

Mrs. Page. I'll have the cudgel hallowed, and hung o'er the altar : it hath done meritorious service.

Mrs. Ford. What think you ? May we, with the *warrant* of womanhood, and the *witness* of a good conscience, pursue him with any farther revenge ?

Mrs. Page. The spirit of wantonness is, sure, scared out of him : if the devil have him not *in fee simple, with fine and recovery*, he will never, I think, in the way of waste, attempt us again.

This Merry Wife of Windsor is supposed to know that the highest estate which the devil could hold in any of his victims was *a fee simple*, strengthened by *fine and recovery*. Shakespeare himself may probably have become aware of the law upon the subject, when it was explained to him in answer to questions he put to the attorney, his master, while engrossing the deeds to be executed upon the purchase of a Warwickshire estate with a doubtful title.

Measure for Measure.

In Act I. Sc. 2, the old lady who had kept a *lodging-house* of a disreputable character in the suburbs of Vienna being thrown into despair by the proclamation that all such houses in the suburbs must be plucked down, the Clown thus comforts her:—

Clo. Come; fear not you: *good counsellors lack no clients.*

This comparison is not very flattering to the bar, but it seems to show a familiarity with both the professions alluded to.

In Act II. Sc. 1, the ignorance of special pleading and of the nature of actions at law betrayed by Elbow, the constable, when slandered, is ridiculed by the Lord Escalus in a manner which proves that the composer of the dialogue was himself fully initiated in these mysteries:—

Elbow. Oh, thou caitiff! Oh, thou varlet! Oh, thou wicked Hannibal! I respected with her, before I was married to her?—If ever I was respected with her, or she with me, let not your worship think me the poor duke's officer.—Prove this, thou wicked Hannibal, or I'll have *mine action of battery* on thee.

Escal. If he took you a box o' th' ear, you might have your *action of slander* too.

The manner in which, in Act III. Sc. 2, Escalus designates and talks of Angelo, with whom he was joined in commission as Judge, is so like the manner in which one English Judge designates and talks of another, that it countenances the supposition that Shakespeare may often, as an attorney's clerk, have been in the presence of English Judges:—

Escal. Provost, *my brother Angelo* will not be altered; Claudio must die to-morrow. * * * If *my brother* wrought by my pity, it should not be so with him. * * * I have laboured for the poor gentleman to the extremest shore of my modesty; but *my brother justice* have I found so severe, that he hath forced me to tell him, he is indeed—JUSTICE.*

Even where Shakespeare is most solemn and sublime, his sentiments and language seem sometimes to take a tinge from his early pursuits,—as may be observed from a beautiful passage in this play,—which, lest I should be thought guilty of irreverence, I do not venture to comment upon:—

---

* I am glad to observe that our "brethren" in America adhere to the old phraseology of Westminster Hall. A Chief Justice in New England thus concludes a very sound judgment:—"My brother Blannerhasset, who was present at the argument, but is prevented by business at chambers from being here to-day, authorises me to say that he has read this judgment, and that he entirely concurs in it."

Angelo. Your brother is a forfeit to the law.
Isabella. ——— Alas! alas!
Why, all the souls that were, were forfeit once;
And He that might the vantage best have took
Found out the remedy: How would you be
If He, which is the top of judgment, should
But judge you as you are? O, think on that;
And mercy then will breathe within your lips,
Like man new made.

(Act II. Sc. 2.)

The Comedy of Errors.

The following is part of the dialogue between Antipholus of Syracuse and his man Dromio, in Act II. Sc. 2:—

Dro. S. There's no time for a man to *recover* his hair, that grows bald by nature.

Ant. S. May he not do it by *fine and recovery?*

Dro. S. Yes, to pay a *fine* for a periwig, and *recover* the lost hair of another man.

These jests cannot be supposed to arise from anything in the laws or customs of Syracuse; but they show the author to be very familiar with some of the most abstruse proceedings in English jurisprudence.

In Act IV. Sc. 2, Adriana asks Dromio of Syracuse, "Where is thy master, Dromio? Is he well?" and Dromio replies—

> No, he's in Tartar limbo, worse than hell:
> A devil in an everlasting garment hath him,
> One whose hard heart is button'd up with steel;
> A fiend, a fairy, pitiless and rough;
> A wolf; nay worse, a fellow all in buff;
> A back-friend, a shoulder-clapper, one that countermands
> The passages and alleys, creeks, and narrow lands:
> A hound that runs counter, and yet draws dry-foot well;
> One that *before the judgment* carries poor souls to hell.
> *Adr.* Why, man, what is the matter?
> *Dro. S.* I do not know the matter; he is *'rested on the case.*
> *Adr.* What, is he arrested? tell me at whose suit.
> *Dro. S.* I know not at whose suit he is arrested, well
> But he's in a suit of buff which 'rested him, that can I tell. * * *
> *Adr.* * * * This I wonder at:
> That he, unknown to me, should be in debt.
> Tell me, was he arrested on a *bond*?
> *Dro. S.* Not on a *bond*, but on a stronger thing:
> A *chain*, a *chain*!

Here we have a most circumstantial and graphic account of an English arrest on *mesne process* ["before judgment"], in an action *on the case*, for the price of a gold chain, by a sheriff's officer, or bum-bailiff, in his buff costume, and carrying his prisoner to a sponging-house—a spectacle which might often have been seen by an attorney's clerk. A fellow-student of mine (since an eminent Judge), being sent to an attorney's office, as part of his legal education, used to accompany the sheriff's officer when making captions on mesne process, that he might enjoy the whole feast of a law-suit from the egg to the apples—and he was fond of giving a similar account of this proceeding,—which was then constantly occurring, but which, like "Trial by Battle," may now be considered obsolete.

As You Like It.

In Act I. Sc. 2, Shakespeare makes the lively Rosalind, who, although well versed in poesy and books of chivalry, had probably never seen a bond or a law-paper of any sort in her life, quite familiar with the commencement of all deeds poll, which in Latin was, *Noverint universi per presentes*, in English, "Be it known to all men by these presents":—

Le Beau. There comes an old man and his three sons,—
Cel. I could match this beginning with an old tale.
Le Beau. Three proper young men, of excellent growth and presence;—
Ros. With bills on their necks,—"*Be it known unto all men by these presents,*"—

This is the technical phraseology referred to by Thomas Nash in his 'Epistle to the Gentlemen Students of the two Universities,' in the year 1589, when he is supposed to have denounced the author of 'Hamlet' as one of those who had "left the trade of *Noverint*, whereto they were born, for handfuls of tragical speeches"—that is, an attorney's clerk become a poet, and penning a stanza when he should engross.

'As You Like It' was not brought out until shortly before the year 1600, so that Nash's *Noverint* could not have been suggested by it. Possibly Shakespeare now introduced the "Be it known unto all men," &c., in order to show his contempt for Nash's sarcasm.

In Act II. Sc. 1, there are illustrations which would present themselves rather to the mind of one initiated in legal proceedings, than of one who had been brought up as an apprentice to a glover, or an assistant to a butcher or a woolstapler:—for instance, when it is said of the poor wounded deer, weeping in the stream—

> " ———— thou mak'st a *testament*
> As worldlings do, giving thy sum of more
> To that which hath too much."

And again where the careless herd, jumping by him without greeting him, are compared to "fat and greasy citizens," who look

> "Upon that poor and broken *bankrupt* there,"—

without pitying his sufferings or attempting to relieve his necessities.

It may perhaps be said that such language might be used by any man of observation. But in Act III. Sc. 1, a deep technical knowledge of law is displayed, howsoever it may have been acquired.

The usurping Duke, Frederick, wishing all the real property of Oliver to be seized, awards a writ of *extent* against him, in the language which would be used by the Lord Chief Baron of the Court of Exchequer—

Duke Fred. Make an *extent upon his house and lands*—

an *extendi facias* applying to house and lands, as a *fieri facias* would apply to goods and chattels, or a *capias ad satisfaciendum* to the person.

So in 'King Henry VIII.' we have an equally accurate statement of the *omnivorous* nature of a writ of PRÆMUNIRE. The Duke of Suffolk, addressing Cardinal Wolsey, says,—

"Lord Cardinal, the King's further pleasure is,
Because all those things you have done of late
By your power legatine within this kingdom
Fall into the compass of a *præmunire*,
That therefore such a writ be sued against you,
To forfeit all your goods, lands, tenements,
Chattels, and whatsoever, and to be
Out of the King's protection."

In the next scene of 'As You Like It' Shakespeare shows that he was well acquainted with lawyers themselves and the vicissitudes of their lives. Rosalind having told "who Time ambles withal, who Time trots withal, who Time gallops withal," being asked, "Who Time stands still withal?" answers—

With lawyers in the vacation; for *they sleep between term and term*, and then they perceive not how Time moves.

Our great poet had probably observed that some lawyers have little enjoyment of the vacation after a very few weeks, and that they again long for the excitement of arguing demurrers and pocketing fees.

In the first scene of Act IV. Shakespeare gives us the true legal meaning of the word "attorney," viz. *representative* or *deputy*. [Celui qui vient à tour d'autrui; Qui alterius vices subit; Legatus; Vakeel.]

Ros. Well, in her person I say—I will not have you.
Orl. Then, in my own person, I die.
Ros. No, faith, *die by attorney*. The poor world is almost six thousand years old, and in all this time there was not any man died in his own person, *videlicet*, in a love-cause.*

* So in 'Richard III.,' Act IV. Sc. 4, the crook-backed tyrant, after murdering the infant sons of Edward IV., audaciously pro-

I am sorry to say that in our time the once most respectable word "attorney" seems to have gained a new meaning, viz. "a disreputable legal practitioner;" so that attorneys at law consider themselves treated discourteously when they are called "Attorneys." They now all wish to be called *Solicitors*, when doing the proper business of attorneys in the Courts of Common Law. Most sincerely honouring this branch of our profession, if it would please them, I am ready to support a bill "to prohibit the use of the word *Attorney*, and to enact that on all occasions the word *Solicitor* shall be used instead thereof."

Near the end of the same scene Shakespeare again evinces his love for legal phraseology and imagery by converting Time into an aged Judge of Assize, sitting on the Crown side:—

> *Ros.* Well, Time is the old JUSTICE that examines all such offenders, and let Time try.

As in 'Troilus and Cressida' (Act IV. Sc. 5) Shakespeare makes Time an *Arbitrator*:—

> "And that old common ARBITRATOR, Time,
> Will one day end it."

---

poses to their mother to marry the Princess Elizabeth, their sister, and wishing the Queen to intercede with her in his favour, says—

> Be the *attorney* of my love to her.

Again in the same play (Act V. Sc. 3) Lord Stanley, meeting Richmond on the field at Bosworth, says—

> I by *attorney* bless thee from thy mother.

Much Ado About Nothing.

It has been generally supposed that Shakespeare, in the characters of Dogberry and Verges, only meant to satirize the ignorance and folly of parish constables—a race with which we of this generation were familiar till the establishment of the metropolitan and rural police; but I cannot help suspecting that he slily aimed at higher legal functionaries—Chairmen at Quarter-sessions, and even Judges of assize,—with whose performances he may probably have become acquainted at Warwick and elsewhere.

There never has been a law or custom in England to "*give a charge*" to constables; but from time immemorial there has been "*a charge to grand juries*" by the presiding judge. This charge, we are bound to believe, is now-a-days always characterised by simplicity, pertinence, and correctness, although, according to existing etiquette, in order that it may not be too severely criticised, the barristers are not admitted into the Crown Court till the charge is over. But when Justice Shallow gave the charge to the grand jury at sessions in the county of Gloucester, we may conjecture that some of his doctrines and directions were not very wise; and Judges of the superior courts in former times made themselves ridiculous by expatiating, in their charges to grand juries, on vexed questions of manners, religion, politics, and political economy. Dogberry uses the very words of the oath administered by the Judges' marshal to the grand jury at the present day:—

Keep your fellows' counsels and your own.
(Act III. Sc. 3.)

If the different parts of Dogberry's charge are strictly examined, it will be found that the author of it had a very respectable acquaintance with crown law. The problem was to save the constables from all trouble, danger, and responsibility, without any regard to the public safety:—

Dogb. If you meet a thief, you may suspect him, by virtue of your office, to be no true man; and for such kind of men, the less you meddle or make with them, why, the more is for your honesty.

2 *Watch.* If we know him to be a thief, shall we not lay hands on him?

Dogb. Truly, by your office you may; but, I think, they that touch pitch will be defiled. The most peaceable way for you, if you do take a thief, is to let him show himself what he is, and steal out of your company.

Now there can be no doubt that Lord Coke himself could not more accurately have defined the power of a peace-officer.

I cannot say as much for the law laid down by Dogberry and Verges in Act IV. Sc. 2, that it was "*flat perjury*" to call a prince's brother villain; or "*flat burglary* as ever was committed" to receive a thousand ducats "for accusing a lady wrongfully." But the dramatist seems himself to have been well acquainted with the terms and distinctions of our criminal code, or he could not have rendered the blunders of the parish officers so absurd and laughable.

Love's Labour's Lost.

In Act I. Sc. 1, we have an extract from the Report by Don Adriano de Armado of the infraction he had witnessed of the King's proclamation by Costard with Jaquenetta; and it is drawn up in the true lawyerlike, tautological dialect,—which is to be paid for at so much a folio:—

> Then for the place where; where, I mean, I did encounter that obscene and most preposterous event that draweth from my snow-white pen the ebon-coloured ink, which here thou viewest, beholdest, surveyest, and seest. * * * Him I (as my ever-esteemed duty pricks me on) have sent to thee to receive the meed of punishment, by thy sweet Grace's officer, Antony Dull, a man of good repute, carriage, bearing, and estimation.

The gifted Shakespeare might perhaps have been capable, by intuition, of thus imitating the conveyancer's jargon; but no ordinary man could have hit it off so exactly, without having *engrossed* in an attorney's office.

Midsummer Night's Dream.

Egeus makes complaint to Theseus, in Act I. Sc. 1, against his daughter Hermia, because, while he wishes her to marry Demetrius, she prefers Lysander; and he seeks to enforce the law of Athens, that a daughter, who refuses to marry according to her father's directions, may be put to death by him:—

> And, my gracious duke,
> Be it so, she will not here, before your grace,
> Consent to marry with Demetrius.
> I beg the ancient privilege of Athens,
> As she is mine, I may dispose of her,
> Which shall be either to this gentleman
> Or to her death, according to our law
> *Immediately provided in that case.*

Commenting on this last line, Steevens observes,—"Shakespeare is grievously suspected of having been placed, while a boy, in an attorney's office. The line before us has an undoubted smack of legal commonplace: Poetry disclaims it."

The precise formula—"In such case made and provided"—would not have stood in the verse. There is certainly no nearer approach in heroic measure to the technical language of an indictment; and there seems no motive for the addition made to the preceding line, except to show a familiarity with legal phraseology, which Shakespeare, whether he ever were an attorney's clerk or not, is constantly fond of displaying.

The Merchant of Venice.

In Act I. Sc. 3, and Act II. Sc. 8, Antonio's bond to Shylock is prepared and talked about according to all the forms observed in an English attorney's office. The distinction between a "single bill" and a "bond with a condition" is clearly referred to; and *punctual payment* is expressed in the technical phrase—"Let good Antonio *keep his day.*"

It appears by Act III. Sc. 3, between Shylock, Salarino, Antonio, and a Jailer, that the action on the bond had been commenced, and Antonio had been arrested on *mesne process.* The trial was to come on before the Doge; and the question was, whether Shylock was entitled to judgment specifically for his pound of flesh, or must be contented with pecuniary damages.

Shylock threatens the Jailer with an action for "escape" for allowing Antonio to come for a short time beyond the walls of the prison:—

> I do wonder,
> Thou naughty Jailer, that thou art so fond
> To come abroad with him at his request.

Antonio is made to confess that Shylock is entitled to the pound of flesh, according to the plain meaning of the bond and condition, and the rigid strictness of the common law of England:—

> *Salarino.* I am sure the Duke
> Will never grant this forfeiture to hold.
> *Antonio.* The Duke cannot deny the course of law.

All this has a strong odour of Westminster Hall.

The trial comes on in Act IV. Sc. 1, and it is duly conducted according to the strict forms of legal procedure. Portia, the PODESTA or judge called in to act under the authority of the Doge, first inquires if there be any plea of *non est factum.*

She asks Antonio, "Do you confess the bond?" and when he answers, "I do," the judge proceeds to consider how the damages are to be assessed. The plaintiff claims the penalty of the bond, according to the words of the condition; and Bassanio, who acts as counsel for the defendant, attempting on equitable grounds to have him excused by paying twice the sum of money lent, or "ten times o'er," judgment is given :—

> *Portia.* It must not be. There is no power in Venice
> Can alter a decree established.
> 'Twill be recorded for a precedent,
> And many an error by the same example
> Will rush into the state. * * *
> This bond is forfeit,
> And lawfully by this the Jew may claim
> A pound of flesh, to be by him cut off
> Nearest the merchant's heart.

However, *oyer* of the bond being demanded, the judge found that it gave "no jot of blood;" and the result was that Shylock, to save his own life, was obliged to consent to make over all his goods to his daughter Jessica and her Christian husband Lorenzo, and himself to submit to Christian baptism.

Shakespeare concludes this scene with an ebullition which might be expected from an English lawyer, by making Gratiano exclaim,—

> In christening thou shalt have *two godfathers* :
> Had I been judge, thou shouldst have had *ten more*,
> To bring thee to the *gallows*, not the *font*—

meaning a jury of twelve men, to find him guilty of the capital offence of *an attempt to murder* ;—whereupon he must have been hanged.

I may further observe that this play, in the last scene of the last act, contains another palpable allusion to English legal procedure. In the Court of Queen's Bench, when a complaint is made against a person for a "*contempt,*" the practice is that before sentence is finally pronounced, he is sent into the Crown Office, and being there "*charged upon interrogatories,*" he is made to swear that he will "answer all things faithfully." Accordingly, in the moonlight scene in the garden at Belmont, after a partial explanation between Bassanio, Gratiano, Portia, and Nerissa, about their rings, some farther inquiry being deemed necessary, Portia says,—

> Let us go in,
> And *charge us there upon inter'gatories,*
> And *we will answer all things faithfully.*

Gratiano assents, observing,—

> Let it be so: the first inter'gatory
> That my Nerissa shall be sworn on is,
> Whether till the next night she had rather stay,
> Or go to bed now, being two hours to day.

The Taming of the Shrew.

In the "*Induction*" Shakespeare betrays an intimate knowledge of the matters which may be prosecuted as offences before the *Court Leet,* the lowest court of criminal judicature in England. He puts this speech into the mouth of a servant, who is trying to persuade Sly that he is a great lord, and that he had been in a dream for fifteen years, during which time he thought he was a frequenter of alehouses:—

> For though you lay here in this goodly chamber,
> Yet would you say, ye were beaten out of door,
> And rail upon the hostess of the house,
> And say you would *present her at the leet,*
> *Because she brought stone jugs, and no sealed quarts.*

Now, in the reigns of Elizabeth and James I., there was a very wholesome law, that, for the protection of the public against "false measures," ale should be sold only in sealed vessels of the standard capacity; and the violation of the law was to be presented at the "Court Leet," or "View of Frankpledge," held in every hundred, manor, or lordship, before the steward of the leet.

Malone, in reference to this passage, cites the well-known treatise of 'Kitchen on Courts,' and also copies a passage from a work with which I am not acquainted—

'Characterismi, or Lenton's Leasures,' 12mo. 1631—which runs thus:—"He [an informer] transforms himselfe into several shapes, to avoid suspicion of *inneholders*, and inwardly joyes at the sight of a blacke pot or *jugge*, knowing that their sale by *sealed quarts* spoyles his market."

In Act I. Sc. 2, the proposal of Tranio that the rival lovers of Bianca, while they eagerly in her presence should press their suit, yet, when she is absent, should converse freely as friends, is illustrated in a manner to induce a belief that the author of Tranio's speech had been accustomed to see the contending counsel, when the trial is over, or suspended,—on very familiar and friendly terms with each other:—

> *Tra.* Sir, I shall not be slack: in sign whereof,
> Please ye, we may contrive this afternoon,
> And quaff carouses to our mistress' health;
> *And do as adversaries do in law,*
> *Strive mightily, but eat and drink as friends.*

This clearly alludes not to the *parties litigating*, who, if they were to eat and drink together, would generally be disposed to poison each other, but to the *counsel* on opposite sides, with whom, notwithstanding the fiercest contests in court, when they meet in private immediately after, it is "All hail, fellow, and well met."

In the first encounter of wits between Katherine and Petruchio, Shakespeare shows that he was acquainted with the law for regulating "trials by battle" between champions, one of which had been fought in Tothill Fields before the judges of the Court of Common Pleas in the reign of Elizabeth.

> *Kath.* What is your crest? a coxcomb?
> *Pet.* A combless cock, so Kate will be my hen.
> *Kath.* No cock of mine; you crow too like *a craven.*
> (Act II. Sc. 1.)

This all lawyers know to be the word spoken by a champion who acknowledged that he was beaten, and declared that he would fight no more:—whereupon judgment was immediately given against the side which he supported, and he bore the infamous name of *Craven* for the rest of his days.

We have like evidence in 'Hamlet' (Act IV. Sc. 4) of Shakespeare's acquaintance with the legal meaning of this word, where the hero says—

> Now, whether it be
> Bestial oblivion, or some *craven* scruple
> Of thinking too precisely on th' event.

All's Well that Ends Well.

In this play we meet with proof that Shakespeare had an accurate knowledge of the law of England respecting the incidents of military tenure, or *tenure in chivalry*, by which the greatest part of the land in this kingdom was held till the reign of Charles II. The incidents of that tenure here dwelt upon are "*wardship of minors*" and "the right of the guardian to dispose of the minor in *marriage* at his pleasure." The scene lies in France, and, strictly speaking, the law of that country ought to prevail in settling such questions; but Dr. Johnson, in his notes on 'All 's Well that Ends Well,' justly intimates his opinion that it is of no great use to inquire whether the law upon these subjects was the same in France as in England, "for Shakespeare gives to all nations the manners of England."

According to the plot on which this play is constructed, the French King laboured under a malady which his physicians had declared incurable; and Helena, the daughter of a deceased physician of great eminence, knew of a cure for it. She was in love with Bertram, Count of Rousillon, still a minor, who held large possessions as tenant *in capite* under the crown, and was in ward to the King. Helena undertook the cure, making this condition:—

Hel. Then shalt thou give me with thy kingly hand
What husband in thy power I will command.

Adding, however:—

Exempted be from me the arrogance
To choose from forth the royal blood of France * * *
But such a one, thy vassal, whom I know
Is free for me to ask, thee to bestow. (Act II. Sc. 1.)

She effects the cure, and the King, showing her all the noble unmarried youths whom he then held as wards, says to her—

Fair maid, send forth thine eye: this youthful parcel
Of noble bachelors stand at my bestowing * * *
———————— thy frank election make:
Thou hast power to choose, and they none to forsake.
(Act II. Sc. 3.)

Helena, after excusing herself to several of the others, comes to Bertram, and, covered with blushes, declares her election:—

Hel. I dare not say I take you; but I give
Me and my service, ever whilst I live,
Into your guiding power.—This is the man.
King. Why then, young Bertram, take her: she's thy wife.

Bertram at first strenuously refuses, saying—

In such a business give me leave to use
The help of mine own eyes.

But the King, after much discussion, thus addresses him:—

It is in us to plant thine honour where
We please to have it grow. Check thy contempt.
Obey our will, which travails in thy good. * * * *
——————————— Take her by the hand,
And tell her she is thine. * * *
Bert. I take her hand. (Act II. Sc. 3.)

The ceremony of marriage was immediately performed, and no penalty or forfeiture was incurred. But the law not extending to a compulsion upon the ward to live with the wife thus forced upon him, Bertram escapes from the church door, and abandoning his wife, makes off for the wars in Italy, where he unconsciously embraced the deserted Helena.

For the cure of the King by the physician's daughter, and her being deserted by her husband, Shakespeare is indebted to Boccaccio; but the wardship of Bertram, and the obligation of the ward to take the wife provided for him by his guardian, Shakespeare drew from his own knowledge of the common law of England, which, though now obsolete, was in full force in the reign of Elizabeth, and was to be found in Littleton.* The adventure of Parolles's drum and the other comic parts of the drama are quite original, and these he drew from his own inexhaustible fancy.

---

* However, according to Littleton, it is doubtful whether Bertram, without being liable to any penalty or forfeiture, might not have refused to marry Helena,—on the ground that she was not of noble descent. The lord could not "disparage" the ward by a *mésalliance*.—Co. Litt. 80a.

The Winter's Tale.

In this play, Act I. Sc. 2, there is an allusion to a piece of English law procedure, which, although it might have been enforced till very recently, could hardly be known to any except lawyers, or those who had themselves actually been in prison on a criminal charge,—that, whether guilty or innocent, the prisoner was liable to pay a fee on his liberation. Hermione, trying to persuade Polixenes, King of Bohemia, to prolong his stay at the court of Leontes in Sicily, says to him—

> You put me off with limber vows; but I,
> Though you would seek t' unsphere the stars with oaths,
> Should yet say, "Sir, no going." * * *
> Force me to keep you *as a prisoner*,
> Not like a guest; *so you shall pay your fees*
> *When you depart*, and save your thanks.

I remember when the Clerk of Assize and the Clerk of the Peace were entitled to exact their fee from all acquitted prisoners, and were supposed in strictness to have a *lien* on their persons for it. I believe there is now no tribunal in England where the practice remains, excepting the two Houses of Parliament; but the Lord Chancellor and the Speaker of the House of Commons still say to prisoners about to be liberated from the custody of the Black Rod or the Serjeant-at-Arms, "You are discharged, *paying your fees.*"

When the trial of Queen Hermione for high treason comes off in Act III. Sc. 2, although the indictment is not altogether according to English legal form, and might be held insufficient on a writ of error, we lawyers cannot but wonder at seeing it so near perfection in charging the treason, and alleging the overt act committed by her "contrary to the faith and allegiance of a true subject."

It is likewise remarkable that Cleomenes and Dion, the messengers who brought back the response from the oracle of Delphi, to be given in evidence, are sworn to the genuineness of the document they produce almost in the very words now used by the Lord Chancellor when an officer presents at the bar of the House of Lords the copy of a record of a court of justice:—

> You here shall swear * * *
> That you, Cleomenes and Dion, have
> Been both at Delphos; and from thence have brought
> The seal'd-up oracle, by the hand delivered
> Of great Apollo's priest; and that since then
> You have not dar'd to break the holy seal,
> Nor read the secrets in 't.

King John.

In Shakespeare's dramas founded upon English history, more *legalisms* might have been expected; but I have met with fewer than in those which are taken from the annals of foreign nations, or which, without depending on locality, "hold the mirror up to nature." This paucity of reference to law or to law proceedings may, perhaps, in part be accounted for by the fact that, in these "Histories," as they were called, our great dramatist is known to have worked upon foundations already laid by other men who had no technical knowledge, and in several instances he appears only to have introduced additions and improvements into stock pieces to revive their popularity. Yet we find in several of the "Histories," Shakespeare's fondness for law terms; and it is still remarkable, that whenever he indulges this propensity he uniformly lays down good law.

Thus in the controversy, in the opening scene of 'KING JOHN,' between Robert and Philip Faulconbridge, as to which of them was to be considered the true heir of the deceased Sir Robert, the King, in giving judgment, lays down the law of legitimacy most perspicuously and soundly,—thus addressing Robert, the plaintiff:—

"Sirrah, your brother is legitimate:
Your father's wife did after wedlock bear him;
And if she did play false, the fraud was hers,
Which fault lies on the hazards of all husbands
That marry wives. Tell me, how if my brother,
Who, as you say, took pains to get this son,
Had of your father claim'd this son for his?
In sooth, good friend, your father might have kept
This calf, bred from his cow, from all the world:
In sooth, he might: then, if he were my brother's,
My brother might not claim him, nor your father,
Being none of his, refuse him. This concludes—
My mother's son did get your father's heir;
Your father's heir must have your father's land."

This is the true doctrine, "*Pater est quem nuptiæ demonstrant.*"

It was likewise properly ruled that the father's will, in favour of his son Robert, had no power to dispossess the right heir. Philip might have recovered the land, if he had not preferred the offer made to him by his grandmother, Elinor, the Queen Dowager, of taking the name of Plantagenet, and being dubbed Sir Richard.

In Act II. Sc. 1, we encounter a metaphor which is purely legal, yet might come naturally from an attorney's clerk, who had often been an attesting witness to the execution of deeds. The Duke of Austria, having entered into an engagement to support Arthur against his unnatural uncle, till the young prince should be put in possession of the dominions in France to which he was entitled as the true heir of the Plantagenets, and should be crowned king of England, says, kissing the boy to render the covenant more binding,

> " Upon thy cheek I lay this zealous kiss,
> *As seal to this indenture of my love.*"

In a subsequent part of this play, the true ancient doctrine of "the supremacy of the crown" is laid down with great spirit and force; and Shakespeare clearly shows that, whatever his opinion might have been on speculative dogmas in controversy between the Reformers and the Romanists, he spurned the ultra-montane pretensions of the Pope, which some of our Roman Catholic fellow subjects are now too much disposed to countenance, although they were stoutly resisted before the Reformation by our ancestors, who were good Catholics. King John declares, Act III. Sc. 1,

> " No Italian priest
> Shall tithe or toll in our dominions;
> But as we under heaven are supreme head,
> So, under heaven, that great supremacy,
> Where we do reign, we will alone uphold,
> Without th' assistance of a mortal hand.
> So tell the Pope; all reverence set apart
> To him and his usurp'd authority.

King Philip. Brother of England, you blaspheme in this.
King John. Though you and all the kings of Christendom
Are led so grossly by this meddling priest,
Dreading the curse that money may buy out,
And by the merit of vile gold, dross, dust,
Purchase corrupted pardon of a man,
Who in that sale sells pardon from himself,—
Though you and all the rest, so grossly led,
This juggling witchcraft with revenue cherish,
Yet I alone, alone do me oppose
Against the Pope, and count his friends my foes."

At the same time, it is clear, from Shakespeare's portraiture of Friar Lawrence and other Roman Catholic ecclesiastics, who do honour to their church, that he was no bigot, and that he regarded with veneration all who seek to imitate the meek example of the divine founder of the Christian religion.

King Henry the Fourth.

PART I.

In Act III. Sc. 1, we have the partition of England and Wales between Mortimer, Glendower, and Hotspur, and the business is conducted in as clerk-like, attorney-like fashion, as if it had been the partition of a manor between joint tenants, tenants in common, or co-parceners.

> *Glend.* Come, here 's the map: shall we divide our right,
> According to our three-fold order ta'en?
> *Mort.* The archdeacon hath divided it
> Into three limits very equally.
> England, from Trent and Severn hitherto,
> By south and east is to my part assign'd:
> And westward, Wales, beyond the Severn shore:
> And all the fertile land within that bound,
> To Owen Glendower:—and, dear Coz, to you
> The remnant northward, lying off from Trent;
> *And our indentures tripartite are drawn,*
> *Which being sealed interchangeably,*
> (A business that this night may execute,)
> To-morrow, cousin Percy, you and I,
> And my good Lord of Worcester, will set forth.

It may well be imagined, that in composing this speech Shakespeare was recollecting how he had seen a deed of partition tripartite drawn and executed in his master's office at Stratford.

Afterwards, in the same scene, he represents that the unlearned Hotspur, who had such an antipathy to "metre ballad-mongers" and "mincing poetry," fully understood this conveyancing proceeding, and makes him ask impatiently,

> "Are *the indentures drawn?* shall we be gone?"

Shakespeare may have been taught that "livery of seisin" was not necessary to a deed of partition, or he would probably have directed this ceremony to complete the title.

So fond was he of law terms, that afterwards, when Henry IV. is made to lecture the Prince of Wales on his irregularities, and to liken him to Richard II., who, by such improper conduct, lost the crown, he uses the forced and harsh figure, that Richard

"*Enfeoffed himself* to popularity" (Act III. Sc. 2).

I copy Malone's note of explanation on this line:—"Gave himself up absolutely to popularity. A feoffment was the ancient mode of conveyance, by which all lands in England were granted in fee-simple for several ages, till the conveyance of lease and release was invented by Serjeant Moor about the year 1630. Every deed of feoffment was accompanied with livery of seisin, that is, with the delivery of corporal possession of the land or tenement granted in fee."

To "sue out livery" is another law term used in this play (Act IV. Sc. 3),—a proceeding to be taken by a ward of the crown, on coming of age, to obtain possession of his lands, which the king had held as guardian in chivalry during his minority. Hotspur, in giving a description of Henry the Fourth's beggarly and suppliant condition when he landed at Ravenspurg, till assisted by the Percys, says,

"And when he was not six-and-twenty strong,
Sick in the world's regard, wretched and low,
A poor unminded outlaw, sneaking home,
My father gave him welcome to the shore:
And when he heard him swear, and vow to God,
He came but to be Duke of Lancaster,
To *sue his livery*, and beg his peace,
With tears of innocency and terms of zeal,
My father, in kind heart and pity mov'd,
Swore him assistance."

King Henry the Fourth,

PART II.

Arguments have been drawn from this drama against Shakespeare's supposed great legal acquirements. It has been objected to the very amusing interview, in Act I. Sc. 2, between Falstaff and the Lord Chief Justice, that if Shakespeare had been much of a lawyer, he would have known that this great magistrate could not examine offenders in the manner supposed, and could only take notice of offences when they were regularly prosecuted before him in the Court of King's Bench, or at the assizes. But although such is the practice in our days, so recently as the beginning of the eighteenth century that illustrious Judge, Lord Chief Justice Holt, acted as a police magistrate, quelling riots, taking depositions against parties accused, and, where a primâ facie case was made out against them, committing them for trial. Lord Chief Justice Coke actually assisted in taking the Earl and Countess of Somerset into custody when charged with the murder of Sir Thomas Overbury, and examined not less than three hundred witnesses against them,—writing the depositions with his own hand. It was quite in course that those charged with the robbery at Gadshill should be "had up" before Lord Chief Justice Gascoigne, and that he should take notice of any of them who, having disobeyed a summons to appear before him, happened to come casually into his presence.

His Lordship is here attended by the tipstaff (or orderly), who, down to the present day, follows the Chief Justice, like his shadow, wherever he officially appears. On this occasion the Chief Justice meeting Sir John, naturally taxes him with having refused to obey the summons served upon him to attend at his Lordship's chambers, that he might answer the information laid against him; and Sir John tries to excuse himself by saying that he was then advised by his "counsel learned in the laws," that, as he was marching to Shrewsbury by the king's orders, he was not bound to come.

Again, it is objected that a Chief Justice could not be supposed, by any person acquainted with his station and functions, to use such vulgar language as that put into the mouth of Sir William Gascoigne when Falstaff will not listen to him, and that this rather smacks of the butcher's shop in which it is alleged that young Shakespeare employed himself in killing calves.

Ch. Just. To punish you by the *heels* would amend the attention of your *ears*; and I care not if I do become your physician.

But "to lay by the heels" was the technical expression for committing to prison, and I could produce from the Reports various instances of its being so used by distinguished judges from the bench. I will content myself with one. A petition being heard in the Court of Chancery, before Lord Chancellor Jeffreys, against a great City attorney who had given him many briefs at the bar, an affidavit was read, swearing that when the attorney was threatened with being brought before my Lord Chancellor, he exclaimed—"My Lord Chancellor! I made him!" *Lord Chancellor Jeffreys*:—"Then will I lay *my* MAKER *by the heels*." A warrant of commitment was instantly signed and sealed by the Lord Chancellor, and the poor attorney was sent off to the Fleet.

I must confess that I am rather mortified by the advantage given to the fat knight over my predecessor in this encounter of their wits. Sir John professes to treat the Chief Justice with profound reverence, interlarding his sentences plentifully with *your Lordship*—"God give your *Lordship* good time of day: I am glad to see your *Lordship* abroad: I heard say your *Lordship* was sick: I hope your *Lordship* goes abroad by advice.

Your *Lordship*, though not clean past your youth, hath yet some smack of age in you, some relish of the saltness of time; and I most humbly beseech your *Lordship* to have a reverend care of your health." Yet Falstaff's object is to turn the Lord Chief Justice into ridicule, and I am sorry to say that he splendidly succeeds,—insomuch that after the party accused of felony has vaingloriously asserted that he himself had done great service to the state, and that his name was terrible to the enemy, the Chief Justice, instead of committing him to Newgate to answer for the robbery at Gadshill, is contented with admonishing him *to be honest*, and dismisses him with a blessing;—upon which Sir John is emboldened to ask the Chief Justice for the loan of a thousand pounds. To lower the law still further, my Lord Chief Justice is made to break off the conversation, in which Falstaff's wit is so sparkling, with a very bad pun.

Ch. Just. Not a penny, not a penny: you are too impatient to bear *crosses*.*

The same superiority is preserved in the subsequent scene (Act II. Sc. 1), where Falstaff being arrested on mesne process for debt at the suit of Dame Quickly, he gains his discharge, with the consent of the Chief

* So bad is this pun that perhaps it may not be useless to remind you that the *penny* and all the royal coins then had impressed upon them the sign of the *cross*.

Justice, by saying to his Lordship—"My Lord, this is a poor mad soul; and she says, up and down the town, that her eldest son is like you:" and by insisting that although he owed the money, he was privileged from arrest for debt, "being upon hasty employment in the king's affairs."

In Act v. Sc. 1, Falstaff, having long made Justice Shallow his butt during a visit to him in Gloucestershire, looks forward with great delight to the fun of recapitulating at the Boar's Head, East Cheap, Shallow's absurdities; and, meaning to intimate that this would afford him opportunities of amusing the Prince of Wales for a twelvemonth, he says—

"I will devise matter enough out of this Shallow to keep Prince Henry in continual laughter the wearing out of six fashions (which is four terms, or *two actions*), and he shall laugh without intervallums."

Dr. Johnson thus annotates on the "*two actions:*"—"There is something humorous in making a spendthrift compute time by the operation of an action for debt." The critic supposes, therefore, that in Shakespeare's time final judgment was obtained in an action of debt in the second term after the writ commencing it was sued out; and as there are four terms in the legal year, —Michaelmas Term, Hilary Term, Easter Term, and

Trinity Term—this is a legal circumlocution for *a twelvemonth.* It would seem that the author who dealt in such phraseology must have been early initiated in the mysteries of *terms* and *actions.*

Shakespeare has likewise been blamed for an extravagant perversion of law in the promises and threats which Falstaff throws out on hearing that Henry IV. was dead, and that Prince Hal reigned in his stead.

> *Fal.* Master Robert Shallow, choose what office thou wilt in the land, 'tis thine.—Pistol, I will double-charge thee with dignities. * * * Master Shallow, my Lord Shallow, be what thou wilt, I am Fortune's steward. * * * Come, Pistol, utter more to me; and withal devise something to do thyself good.—Boot, boot, master Shallow: I know the young King is sick for me. Let us take any man's horses; the laws of England are at my commandment. Happy are they which have been my friends, *and woe unto my Lord Chief Justice!*—Act v. Sc. 4.

But Falstaff may not unreasonably be supposed to have believed that he could do all this, even if he were strictly kept to the literal meaning of his words. In the natural and usual course of things he was to become (as it was then called) "favourite" (or, as we call it, *Prime Minister*) to the new king, and to have all the power and patronage of the crown in his hands. Then, why might not Ancient Pistol, who had seen service, have been made *War Minister?* And if Justice Shallow had been pitchforked into the House of Peers, he might have turned out a distinguished *Law Lord.*—By taking "any man's horses" was not meant *stealing them,* but *pressing* them for the king's service, or appropriating them at a nominal price, which the law would then have justified under the king's prerogative of *pre-emption.* Sir W. Gascoigne was continued as Lord Chief Justice in the new reign; but, according to law and custom, he was removable, and he no doubt expected to be removed, from his office.

Therefore, if Lord Eldon could be supposed to have written the play, I do not see how he would be chargeable with having forgotten any of his law while writing it.

It is remarkable that while Falstaff and his companions, in Act v. Sc. 5, are standing in Palace Yard to see the new king returning from his coronation in Westminster Abbey, Pistol is made to utter an expression used, when the record was in Latin, by special pleaders in introducing a special traverse or negation of a positive material allegation of the opposite side, and so framing an issue of fact for the determination of the jury;—*absque hoc,* "without this that;"—then repeating the allegation to be negatived. But there is often much difficulty in explaining or accounting for the phraseology of Ancient Pistol, who appears "to have been at a great feast of languages and stolen the scraps;"—so that if, when "double charged with dignities," he had been called upon to speak in debate as a leading member of the government, his appointment might have been carped at.

King Henry the Sixth,

PART II.

In the speeches of Jack Cade and his coadjutors in this play we find a familiarity with the law and its proceedings which strongly indicates that the author must have had some professional practice or education as a lawyer. The second scene in Act IV. may be taken as an example.

Dick. The first thing we do, *let's kill all the lawyers.*

Cade. Nay, that I mean to do. Is not this a lamentable thing, that the skin of an innocent lamb should be made parchment?—that parchment, being scribbled o'er, should undo a man? Some say the bee stings; but I say 'tis the bee's wax, for I did but seal once to a thing, and I was never mine own man since.

The Clerk of Chatham is then brought in, who could "make obligations and write court hand," and who, instead of "making his mark like an honest plain-dealing man," had been "so well brought up that he could write his name." Therefore he was sentenced to be hanged with his pen and ink-horn about his neck.

Surely Shakespeare must have been employed to write *deeds* on *parchment* in *court hand*, and to apply the *wax* to them in the form of *seals*: one does not understand how he should, on any other theory of his bringing up, have been acquainted with these details.

Again, the indictment on which Lord Say was arraigned, in Act IV. Sc. 7, seems drawn by no inexperienced hand:—

"Thou hast most traitorously corrupted the youth of the realm in erecting a grammar-school: and whereas, before, our forefathers had no other books but the score and the tally, thou hast caused printing to be used; and *contrary to the king, his crown and dignity*, thou hast built a paper-mill. It will be proved to thy face that thou hast men about thee that usually talk of a noun and a verb, and *such abominable words as no Christian ear can endure to hear.** Thou hast appointed justices of peace, to call poor men before them about matters they were not able to answer. Moreover thou hast put them in prison; and because they could not read, thou hast hanged them, when indeed only for that cause they have been most worthy to live."

How acquired I know not, but it is quite certain that the drawer of this indictment must have had some

* "*Inter Christianos non nominand'*"

acquaintance with 'The Crown Circuit Companion,' and must have had a full and accurate knowledge of that rather obscure and intricate subject—"Felony and Benefit of Clergy."

Cade's proclamation, which follows, deals with still more recondite heads of jurisprudence. Announcing his policy when he should mount the throne, he says:—

> "The proudest peer in the realm shall not wear a head on his shoulders unless he pay me tribute: there shall not a maid be married but she shall pay me her maidenhead ere they have it. Men shall hold of me *in capite;* and we charge and command that their wives be as *free as heart can wish, or tongue can tell.*"

He thus declares a great forthcoming change in the tenure of land and in the liability to taxation: he is to have a poll-tax like that which had raised the rebellion; but, instead of coming down to the daughters of blacksmiths who had reached the age of fifteen, it was to be confined to the nobility. Then he is to legislate on the *mercheta mulierum.* According to Blackstone and other high authorities this never had been known in England; although, till the reign of Malcolm III., it certainly appears to have been established in Scotland; but Cade intimates his determination to adopt it,—with this alteration, that instead of conferring the privilege on every lord of a manor, to be exercised within the manor, he is to assume it exclusively for himself all over the realm, as belonging to his prerogative royal.

He proceeds to announce his intention to abolish tenure in *free soccage*, and that all *men* should hold of him *in capite*, concluding with a licentious jest, that although his subjects should no longer hold in free soccage, "their wives should be as free as heart can wish, or tongue can tell." Strange to say, this phrase, or one almost identically the same, "as free as tongue can speak or heart can think," is feudal, and was known to the ancient law of England. In the tenth year of King Henry VII., that very distinguished judge, Lord Hussey, who was Chief Justice of England during four reigns, in a considered judgment delivered the opinion of the whole Court of King's Bench as to the construction to be put upon the words "as free as tongue can speak or heart can think." See YEAR BOOK, *Hil. Term*, 10 *Hen. VII.*, fol. 13, pl. 6.

Troilus and Cressida.

In this play the author shows his insatiable desire to illustrate his descriptions of *kissing* by his recollection of the forms used in executing deeds. When Pandarus

(Act III. Sc. 2) has brought Troilus and Cressida together in the Orchard to gratify their warm inclinations, he advises Troilus to give Cressida "*a kiss in fee-farm,*" which Malone explains to be "a kiss of a duration that has no bounds,—a fee-farm being a grant of lands in fee, that is for ever, reserving a rent certain."

The advice of Pandarus to the lovers being taken, he exclaims—

> "What! billing again? Here 's—*In witness the parties interchangeably*——"

the exact form of the *testatum* clause in an indenture—"In witness whereof the parties interchangeably have hereto set their hands and seals."

To avoid a return to this figure of speech I may here mention other instances in which Shakespeare introduces it. In 'Measure for Measure,' Act IV. Sc. 1—

> "But my kisses bring again
> *Seals* of love, but *seal'd* in vain:"

and in his poem of 'Venus and Adonis'—

> "Pure lips, *sweet seals* in my soft lips imprinted,
> What bargains may I make, still to be *sealing*?"

King Lear.

In Act I. Sc. 4 the Fool makes a lengthy rhyming speech, containing a great many trite but useful moral maxims, such as—

> Have more than thou showest,
> Speak less than thou knowest, &c.,

which the testy old King found rather flat and tiresome.

> *Lear.* This is nothing, fool.
> *Fool.* Then, 'tis *like the breath of an unfeed lawyer:* you gave me nothing for it.

This seems to show that Shakespeare had frequently been present at trials in courts of justice, and now speaks from his own recollection. There is no trace of such a proverbial saying as "like the breath of an unfeed lawyer,"—while all the world knows the proverb, "Whosoever is his own counsel has a fool for his client."

How unfeed lawyers may have comported themselves in Shakespeare's time I know not; but I am bound to say, in vindication of "my order," that in my time there has been no ground for the Fool's sarcasm upon the bar. The two occasions when "the breath of an unfeed lawyer" attracts notice in this generation are when he pleads for a party suing *in formâ pauperis*, or when he defends a person prosecuted by the crown for high treason. It is contrary to etiquette to take a fee in the one case as well as in the other; and on all such occasions counsel, from a regard to their own credit, as well as from conscientious motives, uniformly exert themselves with extraordinary zeal, and put forth all their learning and eloquence.

I confess that there is some foundation for the saying that "a lawyer's opinion which costs nothing is worth nothing;" but this can only apply to opinions given off-hand, in the course of common conversation,—where there is no time for deliberation, where there is a desire to say what will be agreeable, and where no responsibility is incurred.

In Act II. Sc. 1, there is a remarkable example of Shakespeare's use of technical legal phraseology. Edmund, the wicked illegitimate son of the Earl of Gloster, having succeeded in deluding his father into the belief that Edgar, the legitimate son, had attempted to commit parricide, and had been prevented from accomplishing the crime by Edmund's tender solicitude for the Earl's safety, the Earl is thus made to express a determination that he would disinherit Edgar (who was supposed to have fled from justice), and that he would leave all his possessions to Edmund:—

Glo. Strong and fasten'd villain!
* * * * *
All ports I'll bar; the villain shall not 'scape.
* * * * *
Besides, his picture
I will send far and near, that all the kingdom
May have due note of him;† and of my land,
Loyal and natural boy, I'll work the means
To make thee capable.

In forensic discussions respecting legitimacy, the question is put, whether the individual whose *status* is to be determined is "capable," *i. e.* capable of inheriting; but it is only a lawyer who would express the idea of legitimising a natural son by simply saying—

I'll work the means
To make him capable.

Again, in Act III. Sc. 5, we find Edmund trying to incense the Duke of Cornwall against his father for having taken part with Lear when so cruelly treated by Goneril and Regan. The two daughters had become the reigning sovereigns, to whom Edmund professed to owe allegiance. Cornwall having created Edmund Earl of Gloster says to him—

---

† One would suppose that photography, by which this mode of catching criminals is now practised, had been invented in the reign of King Lear.

"Seek out where thy father is, that he may be ready for our apprehension."

On which Edmund observes aside—

"If I find him *comforting* the King, it will stuff his suspicion more fully."

Upon this Dr. Johnson has the following note:—"He uses the word [comforting] in the juridical sense, for supporting, helping."

The indictment against an accessary after the fact, for treason, charges that the accessary "comforted" the principal traitor after knowledge of the treason.

In Act III. Sc. 6 the imaginary trial of the two unnatural daughters is conducted in a manner showing a perfect familiarity with criminal procedure.

Lear places the two Judges on the bench, viz., Mad Tom and the Fool. He properly addresses the former as "the robed man of justice," but, although both were "of the commission," I do not quite understand why the latter is called his "yokefellow of equity," unless this might be supposed to be a special commission, like that which sat on Mary, Queen of Scots, including Lord Chancellor Audley.

Lear causes Goneril to be arraigned first, and then proceeds as a witness to give evidence against her, to prove an overt act of high treason:

"I here take my oath before this honourable assembly, she kicked the poor king, her father."

But the trial could not be carried on with perfect regularity on account of Lear's madness, and, without waiting for a verdict, he himself sentences Regan to be anatomized:—

"Then, let them anatomize Regan; see what breeds about her heart."

Hamlet.

In this tragedy various expressions and allusions crop out, showing the substratum of law in the author's mind, —*e.g.*, the description of the disputed territory which was the cause of the war between Norway and Poland:—

We go to gain a little patch of ground,
That hath in it no profit but the name.
To pay five ducats, five, I would not farm it,
Nor will it yield to Norway or the Pole
A ranker rate, *should it be sold in fee.* (Act IV. Sc. 4.)

Earlier in the play (Act I. Sc. 1) Marcellus inquires what was the cause of the warlike preparations in Denmark—

And why such daily cast of brazen cannon,
And foreign mart for implements of war?
Why such impress of shipwrights, whose sore task
Does not divide the Sunday from the week?

Such confidence has there been in Shakespeare's accuracy, that this passage has been quoted, both by text writers and by Judges on the bench, as an authority upon the legality of the *press-gang*, and upon the debated question whether *shipwrights*, as well as *common seamen*, are liable to be pressed into the service of the royal navy.*

Hamlet, when mortally wounded in Act v. Sc. 2, represents that Death comes to him in the shape of a sheriff's officer, as it were to take him into custody under a *capias ad satisfaciendum*:—

"Had I but time (as this fell serjeant, Death,
Is strict in his arrest), Oh! I could tell you," &c.

The Grave-diggers' scene, however, is the mine which produces the richest legal ore. The discussion as to whether Ophelia was entitled to Christian burial proves that Shakespeare had read and studied Plowden's Report of the celebrated case of Hales *v.* Petit, tried in the reign of Philip and Mary, and that he intended to

* See Barrington on the Ancient Statutes, p. 300.

ridicule the counsel who argued and the Judges who decided it.

On the accession of Mary Tudor, Sir James Hales, a puisne Judge of the Common Pleas, was prosecuted for being concerned in the plot which placed the Lady Jane Grey for a few days upon the throne; but, as he had previously expressed a strong opinion that the succession of the right heir ought not to be disturbed, he was pardoned and released from prison. Nevertheless, so frightened was he by the proceedings taken against him that he went out of his mind, and, after attempting suicide by a penknife, he drowned himself by walking into a river. Upon an inquisition before the Coroner, a verdict of *felo de se* was returned. Under this finding his body was to be buried in a cross-road, with a stake thrust through it, and all his goods were forfeited to the crown. It so happened that at the time of his death he was possessed of a lease for years of a large estate in the county of Kent, granted by the Archbishop of Canterbury jointly to him and his wife, the Lady Margaret, who survived him. Upon the supposition that this lease was forfeited, the estate was given by the crown to one Cyriac Petit, who took possession of it,—and Dame Margaret Hales, the widow, brought this action against him to recover it. The only question was whether the forfeiture could be considered as having taken place in the lifetime of Sir James Hales; for, if not, the plaintiff certainly took the estate by survivorship.

Her counsel, Serjeants Southcote and Puttrel, powerfully argued that, the offence of suicide being the killing of a man's self, it could not be completed in his lifetime, for as long as he was alive he had not killed himself, and, the moment that he died, the estate vested in the plaintiff. "The felony of the husband shall not take away her title by survivorship, for in this manner of felony two things are to be considered—first, the cause of the death; secondly, the death ensuing the cause; and these two make the felony, and without both of them the felony is not consummate. And the cause of the death is the act done in the party's lifetime, which makes the death to follow. And the act which brought on the death here was the throwing himself voluntarily into the water, for this was the cause of his death. And if a man kills himself by a wound which he gives himself with a knife, or if he hangs himself, as the wound or the hanging, which is the act done in the party's lifetime, is the cause of his death, so is the throwing himself into the water here. Forasmuch as he cannot be attainted of his own death, because he is dead before there is any time to attaint him, the finding of his death by the Coroner is by necessity of law equivalent to an attainder in fact coming after his death. He cannot be *felo de se* till the death is fully consummate, and the death precedes the felony and the forfeiture."

WALSH, Serjeant, *contra*, argued that the felony was to be referred back to the act which caused the death.

"*The act consists of three parts:* the first is the imagination, which is a reflection or meditation of the mind, whether or not it is convenient for him to destroy himself, and what way it can be done; the second is the resolution, which is a determination of the mind to destroy himself; the third is the perfection, which is the execution of what the mind had resolved to do. And of all the parts, the *doing of the act* is the greatest in the judgment of our law, and it is in effect the whole. Then here the act done by Sir James Hales, which is evil, and the cause of his death, is the throwing himself into the water, and the death is but a sequel thereof."

Lord C. J. Dyer and the whole court gave judgment for the defendant, holding that although Sir James Hales could hardly be said to have killed himself in his lifetime, "the forfeiture shall have relation to *the act done* by Sir James Hales in his lifetime, which was the cause of his death, viz., the throwing himself into the water." Said they, "Sir James Hales was dead, and how came he to his death? by drowning; and who drowned him? Sir James Hales; and when did he drown him? in his lifetime. So that Sir James Hales, being alive, caused Sir James Hales to die; and the act of the living man was the death of the dead man. He therefore committed felony in his lifetime, although there was no possibility of the forfeiture being found in his lifetime, for until his death there was no cause of forfeiture."

The argument of the gravediggers upon Ophelia's case is almost in the words reported by Plowden:—

1 *Clo.* Is she to be buried in Christian burial, that wilfully seeks her own salvation?

2 *Clo.* The crowner hath sate on her, and finds it Christian burial.

1 *Clo.* How can that be, unless she drowned herself in her own defence?

2 *Clo.* Why, 'tis found so.

1 *Clo.* It must be *se offendendo;* it cannot be else. For here lies the point: if I drown myself wittingly, it argues an act; and an act hath three branches; it is to act, to do, and to perform. *Argal* she drowned herself wittingly. * * * Here lies the water; good: here stands the man; good. If the man go to this water and drown himself, it is, will he, nill he, he goes; mark you that: but if the water come to him and drown him, he drowns not himself. *Argal* he that is not guilty of his own death shortens not his own life

2 *Clo.* But is this law?

1 *Clo.* Ay, marry is't, crowner's quest law.

Hamlet's own speech, on taking in his hand what he supposed might be the skull of a lawyer, abounds with lawyer-like thoughts and words:—

"Where be his quiddits now, his quillets, his cases, his tenures, and his tricks? Why does he suffer this rude knave now to knock him about the sconce with a dirty shovel, and will not tell him of his action of battery? Humph! This fellow might be in's time a great buyer of land, with his statutes, his recognizances, his fines, his double vouchers, his recoveries: is this the fine of his fines, and the recovery of his recoveries, to have his fine pate full of fine dirt? will his vouchers vouch him no more of his purchases, and double ones too, than the length and breadth of a pair of indentures?"

These terms of art are all used seemingly with a full knowledge of their import; and it would puzzle some practising barristers with whom I am acquainted to go over the whole *seriatim*, and to define each of them satisfactorily.

Macbeth.

In perusing this unrivalled tragedy I am so carried away by the intense interest which it excites, that I fear I may have passed over legal phrases and allusions which I ought to have noticed; but the only passage I find with the *juridical* mark upon it in 'Macbeth' is in Act IV. Sc. 1, where, the hero exulting in the assurance from the Weird Sisters that he can receive harm from "none of woman born," he, rather in a lawyer-like manner, resolves to provide an indemnity, if the worst should come to the worst,—

> "But yet I'll make assurance double sure,
> And *take a bond of fate*;"

—without much considering what should be the penalty of the bond, or how he was to enforce the remedy, if the condition should be broken.

He, immediately after, goes on in the same legal jargon to say,—

"———— our high-plac'd Macbeth
Shall live *the lease* of nature."

But, unluckily for Macbeth, the lease contained no covenants for *title* or *quiet enjoyment*:—there were likewise *forfeitures* to be incurred by the tenant,—with a *clause of re-entry*,—and consequently he was speedily *ousted*.*

Othello.

In the very first scene of this play there is a striking instance of Shakespeare's proneness to legal phraseology:—where Iago, giving an explanation to Roderigo of the manner in which he had been disappointed in not obtaining the place of Othello's lieutenant, notwithstanding the solicitations in his favour of "three great ones of the city," says—

* The lease frequently presents itself to Shakespeare's mind, as in 'Richard III.,' Act IV. Sc. 4—

Tell me what state, what dignity, what honour,
Canst thou *demise* to any child of mine?

This is as clear a reference to *leasing*, as if he had said in full, "demise, lease, grant and to farm let."

"But he, as loving his own pride and purposes,
Evades them with a bombast circumstance
Horribly stuff'd with epithets of war,
And, in conclusion,
Nonsuits my mediators."

"*Nonsuiting*" is known to the learned to be the most disreputable and mortifying mode of being beaten: it indicates that the action is wholly unfounded on the plaintiff's own showing, or that there is a fatal defect in the manner in which his case has been got up: insomuch that Mr. Chitty, the great special pleader, used to give this advice to young barristers practising at *nisi prius*:—"Always avoid your attorney when nonsuited, for till he has a little time for reflection, however much you may abuse the Judge, he will think that the nonsuit was all your fault."

In the next scene Shakespeare gives us very distinct proof that he was acquainted with Admiralty law, as well as with the procedure of Westminster Hall. Describing the feat of the Moor in carrying off Desdemona against her father's consent, which might either make or mar his fortune, according as the act might be sanctioned or nullified, Iago observes—

"Faith, he to-night hath boarded a land carack:
If it prove *lawful prize*, he 's made for ever;"—

the trope indicating that there would be a suit in the High Court of Admiralty to determine the validity of the capture.

Then follows, in Act I. Sc. 3, the trial of Othello before the Senate, as if he had been indicted on Stat. 33 Hen. VII. c. 8, for practising "conjuration, witchcraft, enchantment, and sorcery, to provoke to unlawful love." Brabantio, the prosecutor, says—

> "She is abused, stol'n from me, and corrupted
> By spells and medicines bought of mountebanks;
> For Nature so preposterously to err * * *
> Sans witchcraft could not."

The presiding Judge at first seems alarmingly to favour the prosecutor, saying—

> *Duke.* Whoe'er he be that in this foul proceeding
> Hath thus beguil'd your daughter of herself,
> And you of her, the bloody book of law
> You shall yourself read, in the bitter letter,
> After your own sense.

The Moor, although acting as his own counsel, makes a noble and skilful defence, directly meeting the statutable misdemeanour with which he is charged,—and referring pointedly to the very words of the indictment and the Act of Parliament:—

"I will a round unvarnish'd tale deliver
Of my whole course of love; *what drugs, what charms,*
What conjuration, and what mighty magic
(For such proceedings I am charged withal)
I won his daughter with."

Having fully opened his case, showing that he had used no forbidden arts, and having explained the course which he had lawfully pursued, he says in conclusion:—

"This only is the *witchcraft* I have used:
Here comes the lady—let her witness it."

He then examines the witness, and is honourably acquitted.

Again, the application to Othello to forgive Cassio is made to assume the shape of a juridical proceeding. Thus Desdemona concludes her address to Cassio, assuring him of her zeal as his *Solicitor*:—

"I'll intermingle every thing he does
With Cassio's *suit*: Therefore be merry, Cassio;
For thy *Solicitor* shall rather die
Than give thy cause away."—(Act III. sc. 3.)

The subsequent part of the same scene shows that Shakespeare was well acquainted with all courts, low as well as high;—where Iago asks—

Who has a breast so pure
But some uncleanly apprehensions
Keep leets and law-days, and in *session sit*
With meditations lawful?

Antony and Cleopatra.

In 'Julius Cæsar' I could not find a single instance of a Roman being made to talk like an English lawyer; but in 'Antony and Cleopatra' (Act I. Sc. 4) Lepidus, in trying to palliate the bad qualities and misdeeds of Antony, uses the language of a conveyancer's chambers in Lincoln's Inn:—

"His faults, in him, seem as the spots of heaven,
More fiery by night's blackness; *hereditary*
Rather than *purchas'd*."

That is to say, they are taken by *descent*, not by *purchase*.*

* So in 'the Second Part of Henry IV.,' Act IV. Sc. 4, the King, who had usurped the crown, says to the Prince of Wales—

for what in me was *purchas'd*
Falls upon thee in a more fairer sort.

i.e. I took by *purchase*, you will take by *descent*.

Lay gents (viz., all except lawyers) understand by "purchase" buying for a sum of money, called the price; but lawyers consider that "purchase" is opposed to *descent*—that all things come to the owner either by *descent* or by *purchase*, and that whatever does not come through operation of law by *descent* is *purchased*, although it may be the free gift of a donor. Thus, if land be devised by will to A. in fee, he takes by *purchase*, or to B. for life, remainder to A. and his heirs, B. being a stranger to A., A. takes by *purchase*; but upon the death of A., his eldest son would take by *descent*.

English lawyers sometimes use these terms metaphorically, like LEPIDUS. Thus a Law Lord who has suffered much from hereditary gout, although very temperate in his habits, says, "I take it by *descent*, not by *purchase*." Again, Lord Chancellor Eldon, a very bad shot, having insisted on going out quite alone to shoot, and boasted of the heavy bag of game which he had brought home, Lord Stowell, insinuating that he had filled it with game bought from a poacher, used to say, "My brother takes his game—not by *descent*, but by—*purchase*;"—this being a pendant to another joke Lord Stowell was fond of—"My brother, the Chancellor, in vacation goes out with his gun to kill—time."

Coriolanus.

In this drama, in which we should not expect to find any allusion to English juridical proceedings, Shakespeare shows that he must have been present before some tiresome, testy, choleric judges at Stratford, Warwick, or Westminster,—whom he evidently intends to depict and to satirise,—like my distinguished friend CHARLES DICKENS, in his famous report of the trial of *Bardel* v. *Pickwick,* before Mr. Justice Starey, for breach of promise of marriage. Menenius (Act II. Sc. 1), in reproaching the two tribunes, Sicinius and Brutus, with their own offences, which they forget while they inveigh against Coriolanus, says—

> "You wear out a good wholesome forenoon in hearing a cause between an orange-wife and a posset-seller, and then re-journ the controversy of three pence to a second day of audience. When you are hearing a matter *between party and party,* if you chance to be pinched with the colic, you make faces like mummers, set up the bloody flag against all patience, and in roaring for a ——pot dismiss the controversy pleading more entangled by your hearing: all the peace you make in their cause is, calling both the parties knaves."

Shakespeare here mistakes the duties of the *Tribune* for those of the *Prætor*;—but in truth he was recollecting with disgust what he had himself witnessed in his own country. Nowadays all English judges are exemplary for despatch, patience, and good temper!!!

Romeo and Juliet.

The first scene of this romantic drama may be studied by a student of the Inns of Court to acquire a knowledge of the law of "assault and battery," and what will amount to a *justification.* Although Sampson exclaims, "My naked weapon is out: quarrel, I will back thee," he adds, "Let us take the law of our sides; let them begin." Then we learn that neither *frowning,* nor *biting the thumb,* nor answering to a question, "Do you bite your thumb at us, Sir?" "I do bite my thumb, Sir," —would be enough to support the plea of *se defendendo.**

* To show the ignorance and stupidity of Sir Andrew Aguecheek ('Twelfth Night,' Act IV. Sc. 1) in supposing that *son assault demesne* (or that the Plaintiff gave the first blow) is not a good defence to an action of battery, he is made to say, "I'll have an action of battery against him, if there be any law in Illyria: *though I struck him first, yet it's no matter for that.*"

The scene ends with old Montagu and old Capulet being bound over, in the English fashion, *to keep the peace*,—in the same manner as two Warwickshire clowns, who had been fighting, might have been dealt with at Charlecote before Sir Thomas Lucy.

The only other scene in this play I have marked to be noticed for the use of law terms is that between Mercutio and Benvolio, in which they keenly dispute which of the two is the more quarrelsome;—at last Benvolio,—not denying that he had quarrelled with a man for coughing in the street, whereby he wakened Benvolio's dog that lay asleep in the sun,—or that he had quarrelled with another for tying his new shoes with old riband,—contents himself with this *tu quoque* answer to Mercutio:—

> An I were so apt to quarrel as thou art, any man should buy the *fee-simple of my life* for an hour and a quarter. (Act III. Sc. 1.)

Talking of the *fee-simple of a man's life*, and calculating how many hours' purchase it was worth, is certainly what might not unnaturally be expected from the clerk of a country attorney.*

* So in 'All's Well that Ends Well' (Act IV. Sc. 3) Parolles, the bragging cowardly soldier, is made to talk like a conveyancer in Lincoln's Inn:—"He will sell the *fee-simple of his salvation* * * and *cut the entail from all remainders*."

Poems.

With a view to your inquiry respecting the learning of Shakespeare I have now, my dear Mr. Payne Collier, gone through all his plays,—and I can venture to speak of their contents with some confidence, having been long familiar with them. His Poems are by no means so well known to me; for, although I have occasionally looked into them, and I am not blind to their beauties, I must confess that I never could discover in them (like some of his enthusiastic admirers) the same proofs of surpassing genius which render him immortal as a dramatist. But a cursory perusal of them does discover the propensity to legal thoughts and words which might be expected in an attorney's clerk who takes to rhyming.

I shall select a few instances, without unnecessarily adding any comment.

From Venus and Adonis.

"But when the *heart's attorney* once is mute,
The *client* breaks as desperate in the *suit*."

"Which purchase if thou make for fear of slips,
Set thy *seal-manual* on my *wax-red lips*."

"Her *pleading* hath deserved a *greater fee*."

From the RAPE OF LUCRECE.

"Dim *register* and *notary* of shame."

"For me I force not argument a straw,
Since that *my case is past the help of law.*"

"No rightful *plea* might plead for justice there."

"Hath served *a dumb arrest* upon his tongue."

From the SONNETS.

"When to the *sessions of sweet silent thought*
I *summon up* remembrance of things past."

"So should that beauty which you *hold in lease.*"

"And summer's *lease* hath all too short a date."

"And 'gainst thyself a *lawful plea* commence."

" But be contented; when that fell *arrest*
Without all bail shall carry me away." *

" Of faults concealed, wherein I am *attainted.*"

" Which works on *leases* of short numbered hours."

" *Lord of my love*, to whom in *vassalage*
Thy merit hath my duty strongly knit,
To thee I send this written embassage." †

" And I myself am *mortgag'd.*"

" Why so large cost, having so *short a lease?*" ‡

" So should that beauty, which you *hold in lease*,
Find *no determination.*" §

---

* Death is the sheriff's officer, strict in his arrest, and will take no bail.

† This is the beginning of a love-letter, in the language of a vassal doing homage to his liege lord.

‡ Taxing an overcharge in the attorney's bill of costs.

§ The word "determination" is always used by lawyers instead of "end."

SONNET XLVI.

"Mine Eye and Heart are at a mortal war
How to divide the conquest of thy sight;
Mine Eye my Heart thy picture's sight would bar,
My Heart mine Eye the freedom of that right.
My Heart doth plead that thou in him dost lie
(A closet never pierced with crystal eyes),
But the Defendant doth that plea deny,
And says in him thy fair appearance lies.
To 'cide this title is impannelled
A quest of thoughts, all tenants to the Heart;
And by their *verdict* is determined
The clear Eye's moiety, and the dear Heart's part;
As thus: mine Eyes' due is thine outward part,
And my Heart's right, thine inward love of heart."

I need not go further than this sonnet, which is so intensely legal in its language and imagery, that without a considerable knowledge of English forensic procedure it cannot be fully understood. A lover being supposed to have made a *conquest* of [*i. e.* to have gained by *purchase*] his mistress, his EYE and his HEART, holding as *joint-tenants*, have a contest as to how she is to be partitioned between them,—each moiety then to be held in severalty. There are regular Pleadings in the suit, the HEART being represented as Plaintiff and the EYE as Defendant. At last issue is joined on what the one affirms and the other denies. Now a jury [in the nature of an inquest] is to be impannelled to 'cide [decide] and by their verdict to apportion between the litigating parties the subject matter to be divided. The jury fortunately are unanimous, and after due deliberation find for the EYE in respect of the lady's outward form, and for the HEART in respect of her inward love.

Surely Sonnet XLVI. smells as potently of the attorney's office as any of the stanzas penned by Lord Kenyon while an attorney's clerk in Wales.

Shakespeare's Will.

Among Shakespeare's writings, I think that attention should be paid to his WILL, for, upon a careful perusal, it will be found to have been in all probability composed by himself. It seems much too simple, terse, and condensed, to have been the composition of a Stratford attorney, who was to be paid by the number of lines which it contained. But a testator, without professional experience, could hardly have used language so appropriate as we find in this will, to express his meaning.

Shakespeare, the greatest of British dramatists, appears to have been as anxious as Sir Walter Scott, the greatest of British novelists, to found a family, although he does not require all his descendants to "bear the name and arms of Shakespeare." But, as far as the rules of English law would permit, he seeks to perpetuate in an heir male, descended from one of his daughters (his son having died in infancy, and there being no longer any prospect of issue male of his own), all the houses and lands he had acquired,—which were quite sufficient for a respectable Warwickshire squire. His favourite daughter, Susanna, married to Dr. Hall, an eminent physician, was to be the *stirps* from which this line of male heirs was to spring; and the testator creates an estate in tail male,—with remainders over, which, but for fines and recoveries, would have kept the whole of his property in one male representative for generations to come.

The will, dated 25th March, 1616, a month before his death, having given legacies to various friends and relations, thus proceeds:—

"Item, I give, will, bequeath, and devise unto my daughter, Susanna Hall, for better enabling of her to perform this my will and towards performance thereof, all that capital messuage or tenement, with the appurtenances, in Stratford aforesaid, called the New Place, wherein I now dwell, and two messuages or tenements with the appurtenances, situate, lying, and being in Henley Street, within the borough of Stratford aforesaid; and all my barns, stables, orchards, gardens, lands, tenements, and hereditaments whatsoever, situate, lying, and being, or to be had, received, perceived, or taken, within the towns, hamlets, villages, fields, and grounds of Stratford-upon-Avon, Old Stratford, Bishopton, and Welcombe, or in any of them, in the said county of Warwick; and also all that messuage or tenement, with the appurtenances, wherein one John Robinson dwelleth, situate, lying, and being in the Blackfriars in London, near the Wardrobe; and all other my lands, tenements, and hereditaments whatsoever; to have and to hold all and singular the said premises, with their appurtenances, unto the said Susanna Hall, for and during the term of her natural life; and after her decease, to the first son of her body lawfully issuing, and to the heirs males of the body of the said first son lawfully issuing; and for default of such issue, to the said second son of her body lawfully issuing, and to the heirs males of the body of the second son lawfully issuing; and for default of such heirs, to the third son of the body of the said Susanna lawfully issuing, and to the heirs males of the body of the said third son lawfully issuing; and for default of such issue, the same so to be and remain to the fourth, fifth, sixth, and seventh sons of her body, lawfully issuing one after another, and to the heirs males of the bodies of the said fourth, fifth, sixth, and seventh sons lawfully issuing, in such manner as it is before limited to be and remain to the first, second, and third sons of her body, and to their heirs males; and for default of such issue, the said premises to be and remain to my said niece Hall, and the heirs males of her body lawfully issuing; and for default of such issue, to my daughter Judith, and the heirs males of her body lawfully issuing; and for default of such issue, to the right heirs of me the said William Shakespeare for ever."

In his will, when originally engrossed, there was no notice whatever taken of his wife; but immediately after these limitations he subsequently interpolated a bequest to her in the following words:—

"I give unto my wife my second best bed with the furniture."

The subject of this magnificent gift being only personal property, he shows his technical skill by omitting the word *devise*, which he had used in disposing of his realty.*

---

* The idolatrous worshippers of Shakespeare, who think it necessary to make his moral qualities as exalted as his poetical genius, account for this sorry bequest, and for no other notice being taken of poor Mrs. Shakespeare in the will, by saying that he knew she was sufficiently provided for by her right to dower out of his landed property, which the law would give her; and they add that he *must have been* tenderly attached to her, because (they take upon themselves to say) she was exquisitely beautiful as well as strictly virtuous. But she was left by her husband without house or furniture (except the second best bed), or a kind word, or any other token of his love; and I sadly fear that between William Shakespeare and Ann Hathaway the course of true love never did run smooth. His boyish inexperience was no doubt pleased for a short time with her caresses; but he probably found that their union was "misgraffed in respect of years," and gave advice from his own experience when he said,—

> "Let still the woman take
> An elder than herself; so wears she to him,
> So sways she level in her husband's heart.
> For, boy, however we do praise ourselves,
> Our fancies are more giddy and infirm,
> More longing, wavering, sooner lost and worn,
> Than women's are. * *
> Then let thy love be younger than thyself,
> Or thy affection cannot hold the bent;
> For women are like roses; whose fair flower,
> Being once displayed, doth fall that very hour."

To strengthen the suspicion that Shakespeare was likely not to have much respect for his wife, persons animated by the spirit of the late John Wilson Croker (although Shakespeare's biographers, in the absence of any register of his marriage, had conjectured that it took place in June, 1582), by searching the records of the Ecclesiastical Court at Worcester, have lately made the very awkward discovery that the bond given on grant of the licence for *William*

Having concluded my examination of Shakespeare's juridical phrases and forensic allusions,—on the retrospect I am amazed, not only by their number, but by the accuracy and propriety with which they are uniformly introduced. There is nothing so dangerous as for one not of the craft to tamper with our free-masonry. In the House of Commons I have heard a county member, who meant to intimate that he entirely concurred with the last preceding speaker, say, "I join issue with the honourable gentleman who has just sat down;" the legal sense of which is, "I flatly contradict all his facts and deny his inferences." JUNIUS, who was fond of dabbling in law, and who was supposed by some to be a lawyer (although Sir Philip Francis, then a clerk in the War Office, is now ascertained, beyond all doubt, to have been the man), in his address to the English nation, speaking of the House of Commons, and wishing

Shakespeare to marry *Ann Hathaway* is dated 26th November, 1582, while the entry in the parish register of the baptism of Susanna, their eldest child, is dated 26th May, 1583. As Shakespeare, at the time of this misfortune, was a lad of eighteen years of age, and Miss Hathaway was more than seven years his senior, he could hardly have been the seducer; and I am afraid that she was "no better than she should be," whatever imaginary personal charms may be imputed to her.

to say that the beneficial interest in the state belongs to the people, and not to their representatives, says, "They are only *trustees;* the *fee* is in us." Now every attorney's clerk knows that when land is held in trust, the *fee* (or legal estate) is in the trustee, and that the beneficiary has only an equitable interest. While Novelists and Dramatists are constantly making mistakes as to the law of marriage, of wills, and of inheritance,—to Shakespeare's law, lavishly as he propounds it, there can neither be demurrer, nor bill of exceptions, nor writ of error.

He is no doubt equally accurate in referring to some other professions, but these references are rare and comparatively slight. Some have contended that he must have been by trade a gardener, from the conversation, in the 'WINTER'S TALE,' between Perdita, Polixenes, and Florizel, about raising *carnations* and *gilliflowers*, and the skilful *grafting* of fruit trees. Others have contended that Shakespeare must have been *bred to the sea*, from the nautical language in which directions are given for the manœuvering of the ship in the 'TEMPEST,' and from the graphic description in Henry IV.'s soliloquy of the "high and giddy mast," of the "ruffian billows," of the "slippery shrouds," and of "sealing up the ship boy's eyes." Nay, notwithstanding the admonition to be found in his works, "Throw physic to the dogs," it has been gravely suggested that he must have been initiated in medicine, from the minute inventory of the contents of the apothecary's shop in 'Romeo and Juliet.' But the descriptions thus relied upon, however minute, exact, and picturesque, will be found to be the result of casual observation, and they prove only nice perception, accurate recollection, and extraordinary power of pictorial language. Take the last instance referred to —Romeo's *photograph* of the apothecary and his shop.

> " Meagre were his looks,
> Sharp misery had worn him to the bones :
> And in his needy shop a tortoise hung,
> An alligator stuffed, and other skins
> Of ill-shaped fishes; and about his shelves
> A beggarly account of empty boxes.
> Green earthen pots, bladders and musty seeds,
> Remnants of packthread and old cakes of roses,
> Were thinly scattered to make up a show."
>
> (Act v. Sc. 1.)

Any observing customer, who had once entered the shop to buy a dose of rhubarb, might have safely given a similar account of what he saw, although utterly ignorant of Galen and Hippocrates. But let a non-professional man, however acute, presume to talk law, or to draw illustrations from legal science in discussing other subjects, and he will very speedily fall into some laughable absurdity.

To conclude my summing up of the evidence under

this head, I say, if Shakespeare is shown to have possessed a knowledge of law, which he might have acquired as clerk in an attorney's office in Stratford, and which he could have acquired in no other way, we are justified in believing the fact that he was a clerk in an attorney's office at Stratford, without any direct proof of the fact. Logicians and jurists allow us to infer a fact of which there is no direct proof, from facts expressly proved, if the fact to be inferred may have existed, if it be consistent with all other facts known to exist, and if facts known to exist can only be accounted for by inferring the fact to be inferred.

But, my dear Mr. Payne Collier, you must not from all this suppose that I have really become an absolute convert to your side of the question. ÆNEAS, while in the shades below, for a time believed in the reality of all he seemed to see and to hear; but, when dismissed through the ivory gate, he found that he had been dreaming. I hope that my arguments do not "come like shadows, so depart." Still I must warn you that I myself remain rather sceptical. All that I can admit to you is that you may be right, and that while there is weighty evidence for you, there is nothing conclusive against you.

Resuming the Judge, however, I must lay down that your opponents are not called upon to prove a negative, and that the *onus probandi* rests upon you. You must likewise remember that you require us implicitly to believe a fact, which, were it true, positive and irrefragable evidence in Shakespeare's own handwriting might have been forthcoming to establish it. Not having been actually inrolled as an attorney, neither the records of the local court at Stratford, nor of the superior courts at Westminster, would present his name, as being concerned in any suits as an attorney; but it might have been reasonably expected that there would have been deeds or wills witnessed by him still extant;—and, after a very diligent search, none such can be discovered. Nor can this consideration be disregarded, that between Nash's Epistle in the end of the 16th century, and Chalmers's suggestion more than two hundred years after, there is no hint by his foes or his friends of Shakespeare having consumed pens, paper, ink, and pounce in an attorney's office at Stratford.*

I am quite serious and sincere in what I have written about Nash and Robert Greene having asserted the fact; but I by no means think that on this ground alone it must necessarily be taken for truth. Their statement

* "Three years I sat his smoky room in,
Pens, paper, ink, and pounce consumin'."
Pleader's Guide.

that he had belonged to the profession of the law may be as false as that he was a plagiarist from Seneca. Nash and Robert Greene may have invented it, or repeated it on some groundless rumour. Shakespeare may have contradicted and refuted it twenty times; or, not thinking it discreditable, though untrue, he may have thought it undeserving of any notice. Observing what fictitious statements are introduced into the published "Lives" of living individuals, in our own time, when truth in such matters can be so much more easily ascertained, and error so much more easily corrected, we should be slow to give faith to an uncorroborated statement made near three centuries ago by persons who were evidently actuated by malice.*

---

* In several successive Lives of Lord Chief Justice Campbell it is related that, by going for a few weeks to Ireland as Chancellor, he obtained a pension of 4000*l.* a year, which he has ever since received, thereby robbing the public; whereas in truth and in fact, he made it a stipulation on his going to Ireland that he should receive no pension—and pension he never did receive—and, without pension or place, for years after he returned from Ireland he regularly served the public in the Judicial Committee of the Privy Council, and in the judicial business of the House of Lords. This erroneous statement is to be found in a recent Life of Lord C., which is upon the whole laudatory above due measure, but in which the author laments that there was one fault to be imputed to him which could not be passed over by an impartial biographer, viz., that he had most improperly obtained this Irish pension, which he

What you have mainly to rely upon (and this consideration may prevail in your favour with a large majority of the literary world) is the seemingly utter impossibility of Shakespeare having acquired, on any other theory, the wonderful knowledge of law which he undoubtedly displays. But we must bear in mind that, although he was a mortal man, and nothing miraculous can be attributed to him, he was intellectually the most gifted of mankind, and that he was capable of acquiring knowledge where the opportunities he enjoyed would have been insufficient for any other. Supposing that John the father lived as a gentleman, or respectably carried on trade as one of the principal inhabitants of the town, and that William the son, from the time of leaving the grammar-school till he went to London, resided with his father, assisting him in the management of his houses and land and any ancillary business carried on by him,—the son might have been in the habit of attending trials in the Stratford Court of Record, and when of age he might have been summoned to serve as a juryman there or at the Court Leet; he might have been intimate with some of the attorneys

still continues to receive without any benefit being derived by the public from his services.—Lord C. ought to speak tenderly of *Biographers*, but I am afraid that they may sometimes be justly compared to the hogs of Westphalia, who without discrimination pick up what falls from one another.

who practised in the town and with their clerks, and while in their company at fairs, wakes, church ales, bowling-, bell-ringing-, and hurling-matches, he might not only have picked up some of their professional jargon, but gained some insight into the principles of their calling, which are not without interest to the curious.

Moreover, it is to be considered that, although Shakespeare in 1589 was unquestionably a shareholder in the Blackfriars Theatre, and had trod the boards as an actor, the time when he began to write for the stage is uncertain; and we are not in possession of any piece which we assuredly know to have been written and finished by him before the year 1592. Thus there was a long interval between his arrival in London and the publication of any of the dramas from which my selections are made. In this interval he was no doubt conversant with all sorts and conditions of men. I am sorry to say I cannot discover that at any period of his life Lord Chancellors or Lord Chief Justices showed the good taste to cultivate his acquaintance.* But he must have been intimate with the students at the Inns of

* Although it is said that Shakespeare was introduced to Lord Chancellor Ellesmere, Lord Somers is the first legal dignitary I find forming friendships with literary men.

Court, who were in the habit of playing before Queen Elizabeth at Greenwich, as he took a part in these court theatricals; and the author, in all probability, was present among the lawyers when 'Twelfth Night' was brought out at the Readers' Feast in the Middle Temple, and when 'Othello' was acted at Lord Chancellor Ellesmere's before Queen Elizabeth.

Shakespeare, during his first years in London, when his purse was low, may have dined at the ordinary in Alsatia, thus described by Dekker, where he may have had a daily surfeit of law, if, with his universal thirst for knowledge, he had any desire to drink deeply at this muddy fountain:

"There is another ordinary at which your London usurer, your stale bachelor, and your *thrifty attorney* do resort; the price threepence; the rooms as full of company as a gaol; and indeed divided into several wards, like the beds of an hospital. * * * If they chance to discourse, it is of nothing but of *statutes, bonds, recognizances, fines, recoveries*, audits, rents, subsidies, *sureties, enclosures, liveries, indictments, outlawries, feoffments, judgments, commissions, bankrupts, amercements*, and of such horrible matter."
—*Dekker's Gull's Hornbook*, 1609.

In such company a willing listener might soon make great progress in law;—and it may be urged, that I have unconsciously exaggerated the difficulty to be encountered by Shakespeare in picking up his knowledge of that which I myself have been so long labouring to understand. Many may think that Shakespeare resembles his own Prince Hal, when reformed and become Henry V., who, notwithstanding his revels in East Cheap, and with no apparent opportunities of acquiring the knowledge he displayed, astonished the world with his universal wisdom :

> "Hear him but reason in divinity,
> And, all-admiring, with an inward wish,
> You would desire the king were made a prelate.
> Hear him debate of commonwealth affairs,
> You would say, it hath been all-in-all his study.
> List his discourse of war, and you shall hear
> A fearful battle render'd you in music.
> Turn him to any cause of policy,
> The Gordian knot of it he will unloose
> Familiar as his garter; that, when he speaks,
> The air, a chartered libertine, is still,
> And the mute wonder lurketh in man's ears
> To steal his sweet and honeyed sentences;
> So that the art, and practick part of life,
> Must be the mistress to this theorick."
>
> *Henry V.*, Act I. Sc. 1.

We cannot argue with confidence on the principles which would guide us to safe conclusions respecting ordinary men, when we are reasoning respecting one of whom it was truly said :

> "Each change of many-coloured life he drew,
> Exhausted worlds, and then imagined new;
> Existence saw him spurn her bounded reign,
> And panting Time toiled after him in vain."

And now, my dear Mr. Payne Collier, I must conclude. Long ago, I dare say, you were heartily sorry that you ever thought of taking the opinion of counsel on this knotty point; and at last you may not only exclaim, "I am no wiser than I was," but shaking your head, like old DEMIPHO in 'Terence,' after being present at a consultation of lawyers on the validity of his son's marriage, you may sigh and say, "Incertior sum multò quam dudum."

However, if my scepticism and my argumentation (worthy of Serjeant Eitherside) should stimulate you deliberately to reconsider the question, and to communicate your matured judgment to the world, I shall not have doubted or hallucinated in vain. By another outpouring of your Shakespearian lore you may entirely convince, and at all events you will much gratify,

Your sincere admirer and friend,

(Signed) CAMPBELL.

THE END.

CPSIA information can be obtained
at www.ICGtesting.com
Printed in the USA
LVHW111805190123
737431LV00008B/900

9 783375 138189